DIESEL

THE NIGHTHAWKS BOOK THREE

LISA LANG BLAKENEY

WRITERGIRL PRESS

COPYRIGHT

LISA LANG BLAKENEY

Love reading novels featuring hot alpha men who fall for smart women? Then join MY VIP MAILING LIST at http://LisaLangBlakeney.com/VIP and get a **free** book just for joining!

FOLLOW ME
Follow me on Facebook
Join my Fan Group
Follow me on Amazon
Follow me on Bookbub
Follow me on Instagram

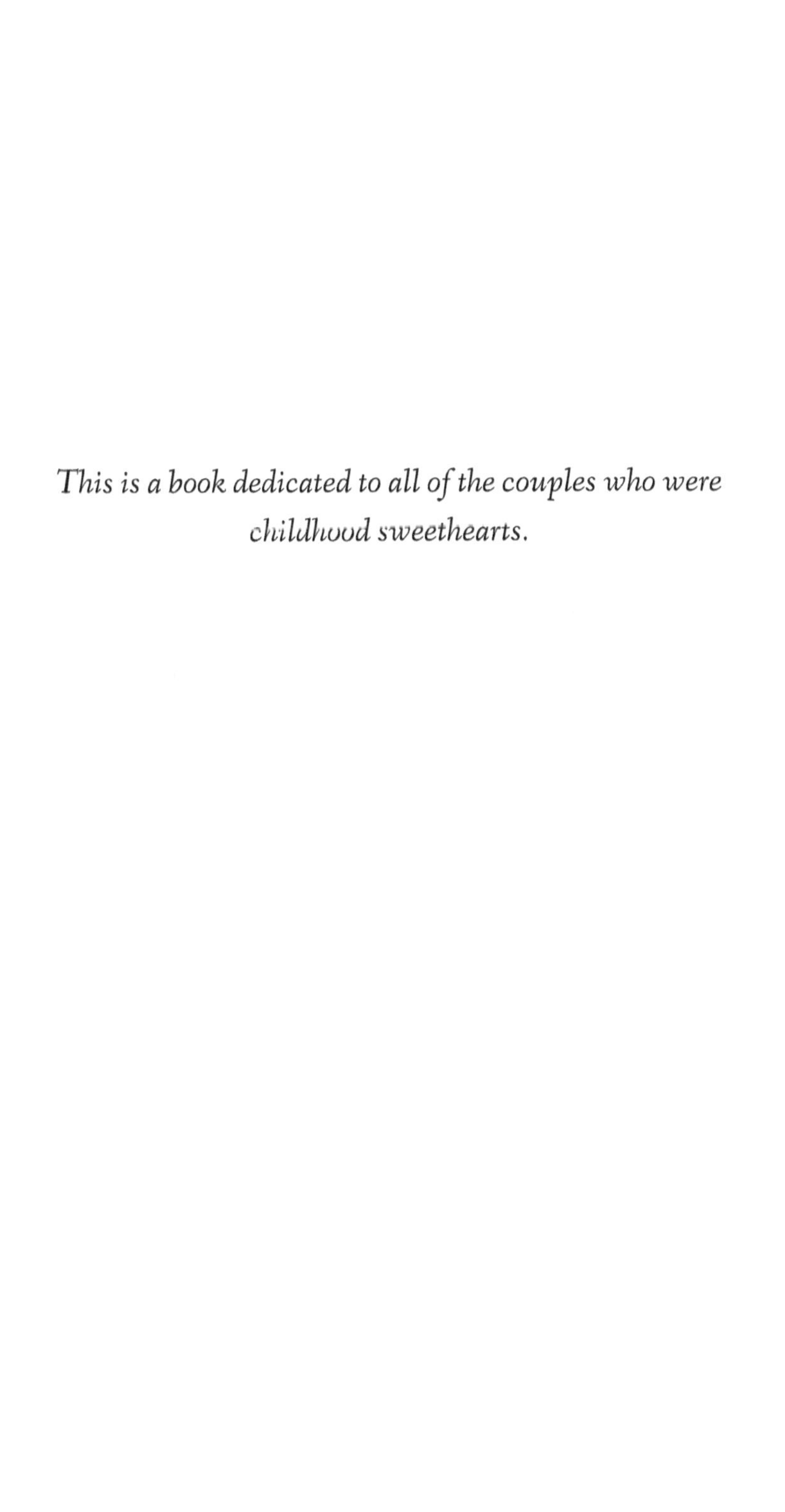

This is a book dedicated to all of the couples who were childhood sweethearts.

The Masterson Series

Devour this addictive series about the possessive bad boy, Roman Masterson, who falls hard and fast for the girl he's promised his family to protect.

Masterson

Masterson Unleashed

Masterson In Love

Masterson Made

Joseph Loves Juliette

Masterson Box Set

Masterson Next Generation Series

The crazy hot fruit doesn't fall far from the tree. Dive into this second generation of Masterson men!

Knox - Knox & Gigi

Bronx - Bronx & Karma

Seven - Coming soon!

The King Brothers Series

Dive into this series of interconnected standalones featuring

3 alpha hot brothers and the women they lay claim to without apology.

Claimed - Camden & Jade

Indebted - Cutter & Sloan

Broken - Stone & Tiny

Promised - All King Brothers

King Brothers Box Set

The Nighthawk Series

Sexy & sweet sports romances set in the professional world of football. All standalones.

Saint - Saint & Sabrina

Wolf - Cooper & Ursula

Diesel - Mason & Olivia

Jett - Jett & Adrienne

Rush - Rush & Mia

Freak - Freak & Willow

Brick - Brick & Kaya

Dak - Coming soon

MASTERSON

Meet Alpha Roman Masterson

Free For A Limited Time!

"Our passion is incredibly intense. The connection between us borders on the possessive. Our feelings are absolutely forbidden. The question now is...what the f*ck are we going to do about it?"

DOWNLOAD NOW

Available exclusively through this link.

A one-click, wow they're sweet, friends-to-lovers story and second chance romance with the golden boy in the NFL.

Two best friends. One fated romance. Diesel is the best friend & boy next door who got away.

From bestselling author, Lisa Lang Blakeney, comes a sweet and sexy standalone **friends to lovers** romance set in the world of professional football.

Olivia

I was the new kid, in a small town, who didn't fit in

when I met Mason Bridgewater. He was big, bossy, and almost knocked me out cold when we first met.

Our friendship grew, and a love grew greater out of that, but now that I've ruined it. Will he ever speak to me again?

Mason

I was the golden boy, from a small town, whose entire world was rocked when I met Olivia Robertson. She talked differently, she acted differently, and I knew pretty quickly that I'd never meet a girl like her again.

Our friendship was unbreakable, our attraction undeniable, and our love unforgettable…or so I thought. The girl who meant everything. Threw me away like I meant nothing. Will she ever love me again?

Diesel can be read as a standalone romance. It is Book Three in The Nighthawk Series.

CHAPTER ONE

OLIVIA

Warm, morning sunlight pours through my new living room window calling undue attention to the layer of fine dust settled around the room. It's obvious that my newly rented and very small Manhattan apartment needs a serious cleaning (and some decent furniture as well), but other than that—it's perfect.

I have been a boarder at a house with three strangers for months, and so that's why I'm super excited that I now have a place to call my own. Flaws and all.

"If I have to lift another box, I'm going to require another bottle of wine as payment."

"You've already had one bottle," I say.

"Like I said, I'm going to need *another*."

"Friends don't charge friends for favors," I retort.

"Says who?"

"Only alcoholics will work for liquor," I jest.

"Again I repeat, *says who?*"

It may not be obvious because of all of the complaining that she's done while helping me move in today, but I know that my friend Kira is ecstatic that I've moved to New York City for my new job. She was one of the first girlfriends I made in college, and although we live very different lives now, there hasn't been a week that's gone by where we haven't kept in touch through either a phone call or email. Always supporting each other in our personal and professional lives.

"Just two more boxes and we're done."

"When are you feeding me?"

"I'll order something now." I chuckle. "What do you want?"

Kira plops herself down on my floor and starts rifling through one of my boxes marked *office*. Inside it is mostly photo albums and assorted business books that I've used throughout my career so far as a sports publicist.

"Wine."

"Very funny."

"We have to toast to your new job. It's good luck."

"Fine, I'll get us some more Pinot, but what about food?"

"Okay, okay. I'm easy like a Sunday morning. Let's just go with pizza. You know how I like it—pineapples and ham."

"First of all, yuck, and second of all, you can get that anytime."

"I can't get New York pizza in Georgia."

"Let's order something else. How about Thai food?"

"What in the ham sandwich? I don't even know what Thai food is."

"Cuisine from the country of Thailand, idiot. Never mind, I'll order you the lime chicken. You're going to love it."

"You get some hotshot new job working publicity for the Nighthawks and now you order shit like lime chicken? Those two things don't even sound like they go together. Lime and chicken." Kira pulls out my high school yearbook. "Ooh, look what we have here!"

"Put that back in the box," I demand.

"No can do. I need a good laugh."

She leafs through the pages.

"Wow, you look exactly the same in all three of these pages. Sweats, sad looking bangs, and a scowl on your face."

"Be quiet—I'd love to see your high school yearbook."

"Ooh, look at this one of Mason." She laughs boisterously. "His face is covered in pie. Where was this?"

"Our town has a Harvest Festival every year right before the high school's big homecoming game."

"Harvest Festival? That sounds so small-town."

Kira is from Atlanta.

"Yeah it is, but it's a great time though. That picture is from the pie throwing booth. He practically had a line around the corner."

I stare at the picture for a moment too long and start to feel a sharp twinge behind one of my ribs.

It's a blaring red flag.

"Seriously, could you just help me unpack my stuff in the kitchen first," I say curtly. "I can unpack the books another day. They're not that important."

Kira's eyes pop up to meet mine.

"I thought you were over Mason?"

"I am," I say looking away from her.

"You aren't," she states in a voice full of

astonishment. "You've been lying your ass off to me these last few years."

"What are you talking about?" I try blowing her off.

"You are a sports publicist. Correction, an NFL publicist. How can you possibly still be affected by me mentioning Mason when you see or hear something about him on the news damn near every day?"

This is my first time working for the NFL. Since graduation, I've been a sports publicist at the college level only. It has enabled me to maintain a safe distance from Mason and anything going on with him in his world, but I wasn't going to allow our past to interfere with my forward momentum. So, I accepted this New York job, believing that I've grown and moved on and that he doesn't matter as much anymore.

Yet it's hitting me right at this very moment that I may have been fooling myself. Turning the channel when they start showing his game highlights. Conveniently hanging up with my mom when she brings up his name or his parents' names. Not looking at any old high school or college photos I have packed away on my phone because he's just about in every single one I've ever taken.

It's crystal clear to me now. I've been purposely avoiding Mason for five years. That's not a sign of a woman who's truly moved on. That's just a sign of someone in a massive amount of denial.

"I'm not affected," I lie.

Kira glares at me for a moment, obviously seeing right through the transparency of my lie; then places the yearbook back in the box and starts playing around with the wires behind my flat screen.

"Did you turn the cable on?" she asks in an effort to change the subject.

"Yeah—they said all I have to do is connect the cable wire and I should be ready to rock and roll."

"Go ahead and order the weird lime chicken thing, and I'll get it up and running. What do you want to watch?"

"Anything."

"I'll find a movie or something. I know that a lot of horror flicks are on this time of year. You want to go old school and watch *The Shining*?"

"Oh hell no," I say as I scroll through the apps on my cell phone. "That's the scariest movie ever made."

"Uh-uh, it was *The Exorcist*."

One thing I've learned about living in New York City is that you can order almost anything you want and have it delivered. Between fresh food delivery services and Amazon, I could probably hide inside of my apartment for a year without ever having to step out to buy anything. I order two lime chicken platters, two bottles of wine, and one bottle of pain reliever to quash the raging headache I feel coming on.

I can't stop thinking about the yearbook.

I can't stop thinking about the festival.

I can't stop thinking about him.

Every single picture in that yearbook holds a tender memory. I can look at each one and remember what was going on in my life when a particular photo was taken and most likely connect it to a memory that includes *him*.

Superstar wide receiver.

Childhood friend.

First love.

A man who I haven't spoken to in five years and probably will never speak to again.

Mason Bridgewater.

Kira and I both sit on the floor and lean our backs against my one tattered sofa. It slides across the wood floor as we lean back.

"You're going to need to put this thing against a wall."

"The picture on the television is distorted."

"Ugh, I'll fix that. You just push the couch back."

We both rise to our feet. Kira goes over to check the settings of my television, and I begin to push the sofa back against the only bare wall available in my living room. She changes the channel a couple of times to test her handiwork and then settles on a sports network.

"Turn that off," I say abruptly. "I thought we were watching a movie."

"Relax, I'm just tweaking the contrast and brightness of the picture."

But it's too late. On the screen, in living color, is a breaking news segment of the very man I've been trying to forget.

"Uh-oh," Kira says looking at me. "You're up shit's creek now. What are you going to do?"

"I don't know," I practically whisper in shock.

What I've just heard has totally rocked my entire world.

American Sports Network

BREAKING NEWS…
Diesel Powered or Dead Weight?

In a surprise announcement, an interesting and seemingly closed door deal has been cut seconds away from the player trade deadline. Arizona Cardinals wide receiver, Mason Bridgewater, has just been traded for a third round draft pick to the New York Nighthawks.

Bridgewater started his career as the fastest wide receiver in the league, but unfortunately hasn't played a full season since his rookie year due to various reasons including injury. Rumors about the receiver not getting along with his quarterback have also plagued him over the last few seasons, and it may be the number one reason why he's been traded.

Will this be the fresh start that the talented wide receiver has been looking for? Or will this be yet another mediocre year for the player nicknamed Diesel, who single-handedly carried the offense of Georgia Union University to a national championship?

One thing is for sure, New York is giving Bridgewater the second chance that he so desperately needs to prove that he is worth his four year, forty million dollar contract. Let's just hope he doesn't blow it. Second chances are hard to come by.

FIRST QUARTER

"M a!" I let out a bloodcurdling scream, not because I'm frightened or hurt, but because I'm startled. My mother just playfully whacked the backs of my thighs with a damp towel, and I didn't see it coming. "You scared the bejesus out of me."

"Wake up and stop daydreaming," she says to me. "And don't say bejesus."

"I'm already awake, Ma. You didn't have to scare me half to death."

"I was simply getting your attention. You're staring out the window like a zombie."

"Maybe because I'm bored," I say to my mother as if it should be obvious.

My mom wipes her sweaty forehead with an old

Christmas hand towel she found in a box somewhere, sighs, and then gives me what I not-so-fondly call the death stare.

"I can't believe that you're *actually* saying that you're bored?"

"Well kind of," I admit with regret. I can already tell by my mom's tone of voice, and her heavy pronunciation of the *c* sound in the word actually, that I just made a big mistake using the *b* word. Saying the word *bored* is tantamount to saying a curse word like shit or damn in my house.

"There are about a dozen or so boxes in this kitchen that you could help me finish unpacking, Miss Olivia Robertson. That should solve all of your *I'm bored* problems."

See what I mean?

"You can start with the Tupperware in that big box over there." She points toward the largest cardboard box I think I've ever seen. "Unpack those first, and then rinse them out."

"Mom, it's blazing hot in here," I whine. "I can literally see condensation dripping down the walls."

"Olivia, I have a million things to do if this house is ever going to look like human beings live in it before I start my new job. If you're going to help me then help. If all you're going to do is complain, then grab yourself a bottle of water and go outside."

"Go outside where?"

"I don't know. Find some kids to play with." She makes a shooing gesture with her hands. "There are plenty of children in this neighborhood. It's part of the reason why we moved here."

My mother and I have just moved into our brand new "gingerbread" looking house in the very hot town of Bear Springs, Georgia, and so far I don't like anything about this place at all.

First of all, it's small. You can literally walk from the ice cream shop to the library and then to the airport in less than fifteen minutes. Even though I can't actually confirm that, I heard some old lady say it in the gas station mart last night while Mom was playing her lotto numbers.

"If you care one iota about yourself, put on a new shirt before you leave. I've never seen a little girl like you in my life. I know you adore that weird little singing group, Thunder Road, but you've worn that ratty T-shirt of theirs at least three days in a row and I'm sure it reeks."

Weird singing group?

I run over to my mom, lift my arm up, and shove my armpit toward her face.

"Do I reek?" I ask through a fit of laughter.

"Ick!" She turns up her nose. "Why do you have to act like a little boy all of the time? And please go wipe your face down with a paper towel for goodness sake. You're sweating like a country fair pig."

That's another thing I don't like about my new town. It's hot as a frying pan here. Nothing like the gorgeous, seasonal weather we have in New Jersey. Sure, our summers back home are humid, but they're nothing like this. Plus we have the beach. Every family from Jersey goes to the beach, and despite the name of where we live now, there's no actual body of water—or bears—here in Bear Springs. All I see here are trees, flowers, and the biggest bugs on the planet.

I huff loudly as I wipe myself down with a moistened paper towel. I don't want to go outside and make new friends. Not when the ones I have back in New Jersey are perfectly fine. I don't even know anybody here, and I won't until I start school in the fall. So who am I going to hang with?

My mother gives me the humongous box of Tupperware and a few careful looks as a warning. If I don't leave the kitchen in the next few seconds, I'll be matching plastic bins with colored lids for the next two hours of my life. No, the rest of my life.

"Is the cable set up yet?" I ask in a last ditch

effort to find something else to do inside of the house that doesn't involve plastic containers.

"No."

"So no TV?"

"You can watch channels ABC, CBS, and NBC if you use the new antennae I bought. You'll have to look for it though. I'm pretty sure I packed it in one of those boxes in the corner over there."

"Three channels!"

"Yes, three channels. That's what we did in my day, and we were just fine. If there wasn't anything to watch on those three channels then you went outside and played. Something you should seriously consider doing if you don't want to help me unpack."

My mom is not just "old school" but she's old. She is always one of the oldest parents at back to school night, and I bet you can tell by that prehistoric suggestion she just made.

I was what you call a *miracle baby*, also known as a *turkey baster baby*. My mom suffered three miscarriages and one divorce because she wanted to have a baby so badly, and finally ended up with me when I was conceived in a doctor's office via artificial insemination. So that's why she always makes references to stuff that she grew up doing that practically no other mother I know did.

I haven't met a single adult but her that grew up watching only three television channels. I'm not even sure that I believe her. Is that even possible? I can't imagine a child subjected to choices on three stations only. That is cruel and unusual punishment.

"I'm going outside then, but don't say anything if I'm kidnapped by aliens or something."

"What?" she says distracted by a bug the size of my fist flying around in our new kitchen.

"Kidnapped by aliens," I say again. Making sure to emphasize the *K* sound.

"Olivia, you are the most dramatic eleven year old child I've ever seen. Unless you're abducted by little green men from Mars, would you just make sure to come home before it gets dark?"

That'll be easy enough. There isn't diddly-squat to do around here. We live in what my mom described as a cul-de-sac, in a development called Bear Springs Village. At the far end of the horseshoe area of houses is a well manicured field with a playground on the side of it. There are three big swings, one kiddie swing, a massive jungle gym, and two tennis courts.

There's a woman and a small child sitting side by side on the swings and a couple of kids playing on the jungle gym. The courts are empty, but that's probably because it's midday and the heat is becoming unbearable.

The only thing that looks remotely interesting going on is a game of touch football on the grassy field. I love football. Unlike most of the other girls in my grade I don't care much about princess stories or makeup. Instead, I used my time during recess to play football with some of the boys in my class.

"Can I play?" I ask a group of boys who look mostly around my age.

"You?" A gigantic boy, with wild dirty blond hair, and a menacing look on his face asks. He seems kind of intimidating, but I'm not going to let him see me sweat. Jersey girls like me are tough as nails.

"Yeah, me. Haven't you ever seen a girl play football before?" I challenge using the toughest Jersey accent that I can muster.

"Nope, can't say that I have."

"I guess there's a first time for everything."

The big kid plops himself down on the grass over on the edge of the field, folds his arms together, and then gives me a stern look.

"Not on my watch."

CHAPTER FOUR

OLIVIA

I really don't like this kid. I don't like the weird southern twang—as my mom calls it—in his voice, his bushy mane of dirty blond curls that kind of covers his left eye, or the new look on his face. It's a look that I've seen from boys before. Boys who don't think a girl should play football.

Dumb boys.

"So you're not going to play if she plays, Mason?" One of the other boys asks with concern.

What, do they worship this kid or something?

"*She* is Olivia," I say with my arms crossed in front of me.

"What?" the kid asks with confusion.

"I said that my name is Olivia. Don't refer to me as she."

"Sheesh, all right. It's just a pronoun, dude."

"Where are you from?" the mean boy they call Mason asks. "Your accent is strange."

He asks the question staring very obviously at the front of my T-shirt, and I'm not sure if he's staring because of the words printed across it or the fact that I have pretty developed boobs for a girl my age. He should mind his own business if it's because of the latter. My mom says that beautiful boobs run in the family, and I should learn to embrace them.

"New Jersey."

"I've never met anyone from New Jersey."

"Well, now you have."

"So people who live in New Jersey don't have their own pro team right?"

"Not exactly," I say.

"That sucks," one of the other boys chimes in.

"I don't get it. What do you all do? Do you root for the Eagles, the Giants, or the Jets?"

"The Giants and Jets are New York teams, so people in Northern New Jersey usually root for them," I say in a patronizing tone. These so-called football fans should know this already. "I'm from South Jersey, which is very close to Philadelphia, so we are all Eagles' fans."

Duh.

"I think she just talked to us like we're idiots."

"Too bad for you that they suck this year."

I ignore the last comment partly because I've made it a habit not to respond to jerks, but mostly because he's right. My team had a little trouble last season, but that's just part of being a sports fan. Sometimes your team is going to have an awesome year and sometimes they stink. What matters most is loyalty.

"Why are you staring at my shirt?" I finally ask.

Sick of the mean boy's gawking.

"I'm just wondering if you actually listen to Thunder Road?"

The other boys start to laugh.

"Yes," I say proudly. "Every chance I get."

"But they suck."

"No, they don't!" I exclaim in horror. "Did your mom drop you on your head as a baby or something? Take what you said back right now."

"They're a made-up boy band who don't make real music. How can you like them? Even their name is bad."

"That's the name of the street they grew up on!"

Everyone laughs at me again.

"You don't honestly believe that, do you? They make up all of that stuff."

I roll my eyes at the whole lot of them but I really want to cry. Everyone back home loves Thunder Road. Everyone back home is normal. Why am I stuck here with these weirdos, this heat, and all of these dang bugs?

"Good thing what you think doesn't matter to all the millions of loyal Thunder Road fans all over the world."

Two girls in matching green Bermuda shorts and pink polo tops walk over to us but are looking straight at Mason with goo-goo eyes as they approach.

"Hi, Mason," they both greet him in sugary unison.

"Hey." He looks disinterested.

"My parents are throwing me a birthday party next Friday at four. My mom wouldn't allow me to bring invitations to school so that the uninvited kids won't get their feelings hurt, so I'm inviting you now. You're going to come, right?"

"Oh, um, I have a big game next weekend."

"*All* weekend?"

Mason looks uncomfortable by the forwardness of the girl. I suspect it has something to do with how southern boys are raised to be all mannerly and stuff, so I take it upon myself to help him out. Why I help, I don't know. I guess I do it because he looks like he needs it.

"Obviously, he has practice on Friday night and then plays Saturday," I interject. "Guess you girls don't know too much about football."

Mason cracks a smile and both girls look at me with serious attitudes.

"And who are you?"

The birthday girl looks me up and down as if my outfit or maybe my smell offends her. I should introduce her to my mother. They would definitely get along.

"This is Jersey girl," Mason says.

"Jersey girl?"

"The name is Olivia," I make sure to correct them both. My mom always says that all you have in this world is your name and your good reputation, so it's important to protect them both. "I'm *from* the great state of New Jersey."

"You're the new girl who moved into the Bitterman house over in Bear Springs Village?"

"Um, I guess. Who are the Bittermans?"

"The nice family that used to live in your house next door to Mason."

I whip my head around in shock and find that his

face reflects what I'm feeling in the pit of my stomach.

"We're neighbors!" We both exclaim in horror.

Why couldn't it be some nice old couple who live next door who talk about the "old days" and give me fresh baked oatmeal cookies? Why does it have to be this oversized, golden-haired, Thunder Road hater?

"And doesn't your mom work at the university?" *What the!*

Does this annoying girl, dripping in preppy pink and green clothing, know everything about everyone in this town?

"How do you know that?" I ask.

"Everyone's parents work there."

"Or attended there."

"Well I'm not going there," I announce firmly.

"You don't know where you're going to end up," Mason says. "That's a long ways off."

"I'm going to end up at whatever school has girls on the football team, and most likely that's going to be a school back up north where I'm from."

There's shared laughter among all of them. Everyone, except Mason. He just stares at me with the oddest look on his face. He either finds me interesting or ridiculous.

"Sorry to break it to you, but there's no girl's football team at any college I've ever heard of," one of the kids says.

"There will be tons of girls playing by the time I get there," I say with certainty. "And I'm going to be one of the stars on the team."

They all laugh at me again.

"Mason is the one who's going to be a star from this town. Everyone knows that. There are already a few college scouts that come by to check out some of his games. Bet you can't say the same."

These kids are really starting to annoy me.

"Are we playing or not?" I ask while balling up my fists. Determined to show them my skills on the football field.

"Don't mind them. You just have to understand that things are a little different down here," Mason says as he looks at my clenched fists. "Girls don't play football in Georgia."

"That's dumb."

"Not really. They don't let girls play for the same reasons I'm not going to play with you right now. I'm twice your size, twice your weight, and you could get hurt. What's dumb about that?"

"I guess the girls must be tougher up north," one

of the girls sarcastically says as the rest of them chime in with a few snickers.

"I guess we are," I respond. Sassing them back.

"Aw, let her play, Mason," one of the boys says.

"I'm not stopping her from playing," Mason says holding his hands up. "Y'all can play with her if you want. *I'm* just not playing."

"But you have to play too."

"Yeah, there's no game without you in it."

"Let her try, Mason. Bet she'll quit after two plays anyway."

I'm hopeful that these nitwits will come to the only conclusion that makes sense—let me play—so I can show them the speed of a Jersey girl, but I can see that it all depends on what my new next door neighbor decides. There will be no game today without his approval or participation. That's pretty clear.

"You sure you want to do this?" He looks at me with some apprehension.

"Yep."

"And you've played with boys before?"

"Yes! A million times."

"All right, Jersey girl, just don't go ratting us out to your momma if you get smashed."

I roll my eyes.

This boy thinks way too highly of himself.

"Deal."

CHAPTER FIVE

What a craptastic mess this is. My mom has probably told me a million times that I don't know my own strength. I guess that's why she's the mom, and I'm the idiot son, because as usual, she's one hundred percent right.

Jersey girl is stretched out on the grass, completely on her back, with her eyes closed and her fists clenched. Her puffy dark brown ponytails are covered in grass clippings, and she's biting down on her bottom lip as if she's in pain or embarrassed—although she shouldn't be.

It was all my fault.

I was too rough when I ran in for the touchdown. Honestly, I didn't know it was her behind me at first. I had the ball and was in a zone, and all I felt was someone gaining on me as I ran. As fast as her feet were flying, I thought it was Pete. After me, he's the fastest runner out of us all, so when someone grabbed my shirt from behind, I immediately assumed it was him and I yanked away. I yanked so hard that she went flying to the ground right onto her tailbone and hitting the back of her head on the field.

"Jersey girl!" I snap my fingers in an attempt to get her to open her eyes. If I have to get my mom involved in this, I'll be grounded for a week. "Wake up."

"Dude, she's not moving."

"Yo, she's sweating really badly too. You think she's dying?"

"Of course not, idiot. Mason may have flung her around like a rag doll, but he didn't kill her."

"I knew this was a bad idea."

"Really?" I counter giving all of my friends the screw face. "Because y'all were the ones who begged me to let her play."

"You better go get your dad, Mason."

"No way!" I say to my friends. My dad is worse than my mom. If I ask him for help I'll be grounded for a month for sure. He's told me repeatedly. *Real men don't hit, shove, bite, or call girls nasty names. If I catch you doing it, you'll regret it.*

"She probably just needs a minute to shake it off. That's what we do at practice. Pete, go walk to the mart and buy her a bottle of water," I demand. "We already drank out of these bottles."

"I need fifty more cents."

I reach in my pocket and dig out thirty-five cents.

"This is all I've got. Just be nice to the lady up front, and she'll give it to you even if you're short the full amount."

"Dude, that old lady is nice to you because she thinks you're twenty years old."

My friends chuckle as if there's time for jokes.

"Just do it before we all get in trouble," I command. Concerned that my new neighbor is still staying plastered to the ground, clenching and unclenching her fists and not saying a word.

I'm a little frightened that I've actually hurt her, and I feel like a jerk about it. I knew better than to play football with a girl. I don't know how to play the game gently. I never have. I catch the ball and then I stiff-arm or knock down anyone who's in my way to get to the end zone. My dad has been saying for years that I could easily play a position on the offensive line because of my size and toughness, but there's no glory in that.

I was born to run.

So a wide receiver I will be.

"Hey, Jersey girl, are you in pain?" I ask.

"Not dy rain."

"Not dy rain? I can't understand you."

I'm never going to see the outside world again if this girl has a concussion.

It seems to take her a lot of effort to speak, but she gets it out clearer this time.

"Not. My. Name."

"You mean when I call you Jersey girl?"

She flops her fist heavily against the grass.

"Yesss," she hisses.

I smile to myself. *Oh, she's angry.* It's so uncommon for kids to get mad at me, I forgot what it looks like. It's kind of ... refreshing.

"Sorry, um—" I think hard for a moment. I know she told us her name. It's just that sometimes I forget things. "Olivia."

Pete finally comes running back with a bottle of spring water. Before he can give it to her, I grab it from him and offer it to her myself.

"Here, drink this," I tell her.

She angrily nods her head back and forth no.

"You can't just lie here forever," I say.

"I'm gettin' up."

I offer her my hand to help her stand. I can tell

that she's trying mighty hard not to show that something is hurtin' on her. I can respect that. This girl is no punk. And not that it means squat right now, but I can' t help but notice that one of her eyes is slightly larger than the other. I've never seen that before. It's kind of unique. Between her northern accent, her love for football, and her mismatched eyes—Jersey girl has got to be one of the most interesting girls I think I've ever seen in Bear Springs.

"What school are you going to?" I ask. All of a sudden, I want to know more about her. There's only one public school for kids our age in Bear Springs, but her parents may be sending her to a private school.

"Bear Springs Middle School."

"That's where we all go too," I say. Doing my best to keep the excitement out of my voice.

"You're in middle school?" she asks in a voice full of disbelief.

I'm used to the question.

"I'm big for my age," I tell her.

"You definitely are." She brushes some dirt off of the back of her shorts and finally takes a swig of the water. "You're faster and stronger than any boy I've ever met. I feel like a Diesel truck just ran me over."

"I warned you," I say shrugging my shoulders in a *I told you so* kind of way.

"Get over yourself," she retorts. "I feel better already. You guys want to keep playing or what?"

Man, this girl is tough.

"Yeah, but we're not going to play."

"Why not?" she asks.

"Gonna ride you back home on my bike first."

CHAPTER SIX

"Mason, you're going to let *her* ride on your bike?" Kelly rudely asks as if I'm doing something wrong.

And she wonders why I don't want to go to her birthday party. She's been way too bossy and clingy ever since I kissed her on the lips during a game of truth or dare in the fifth grade. Girls are crazy. Especially ones like Kelly.

"I'm not going home," Jersey girl says.

"Why not?"

"My mom's going to make me unpack the entire house if I go home, and I don't feel like it."

"Not when I tell her that you probably have a concussion."

"And how would you know that?"

"My dad works at the university too. He's a trainer with the athletic department, and he sees this kind of stuff every day. He taught me what to look for. Now hop on the back and keep your feet out of the spokes."

"I can walk, thank you very much."

"I knocked you down hard. You shouldn't walk home in this heat."

"You better drop me off in the front and run then, because my mom's going to kill you when she finds out you're the one who damaged my head."

"You shouldn't have played with them!" Kelly says.

"And we made a deal. You agreed that you weren't going to rat us out to your folks," I add.

"You're scared now, aren't you?" she asks with a sinister smile on her face.

That's when I notice something else about Jersey girl. She has two buck teeth in the front of her mouth that you can't help but stare at when she grins. I wonder if her friends back home called her bucky.

"Nope. I'm never scared."

"You should be."

"I have to meet your mom sometime. We *are* next door neighbors after all."

"You'd be surprised. There are people from my

block back home that I swear I only saw two times a year. Halloween and Christmas. Neighbors don't have to talk to each other at all if they don't want to."

"This is Bear Springs, not New Jersey. We talk to each other down here. In fact, I bet that my mom will have invited your mom for coffee by next week, probably sooner."

"My mom doesn't do small chat or coffee. She's a single mother with a full-time job."

"Trust me, my mom won't take no for an answer."

"That might be kind of nice if it happens. My mom doesn't have any friends down here just like me."

"Correction, you have one friend now."

Jersey girl tries to hide what I think is a smile as she quietly climbs up on the seat behind me. I ride a souped-up mountain bike that my dad altered to accommodate my large size. She grabs the sides of my shirt to hold herself steady and tries her best not to lean into me. I want her to though, so I make sure to take the long way home over rough road.

"Where are we going?"

"Just showing you around the neighborhood for a minute."

"It literally is only going to take you a minute to show me. This town is so small."

"You're not happy that you moved here, are you?" I ask as I huff uphill.

"How did you know?" she responds sarcastically.

I keep riding. Pointing out to her some of the little nooks and crannies of my town. Maybe once she gets to know the place, she'll change her mind. Maybe once she sees all of the cool places here, she won't be so sad. I think seriously for a moment about showing her my hideaway by the creek but then change my mind. There's plenty of time for that. We've got all summer.

"This is Bear Creek," I tell her.

"Oh, so there is actual water around here."

"You like to swim?"

She doesn't answer me right away.

I keep pedaling us on the path by the creek.

"Yes, I like the water." She seems to reluctantly admit. "You know it's kind of pretty out here."

"Yeah."

I swerve my bike around the bend a little too fast, and we almost wipe out because I'm not used to the extra weight of another person on my bike. We're saved just in the nick of time she leans slightly to the opposite side, balancing our weight and saving us from falling in the middle of the road. She's not like your average girl from around here, she's clearly been on someone's bike before—and now that I know that, I ride faster.

"Hold on tight," I tell her.

She shrieks with joy as I pedal faster down the slope of one of my favorite bike paths.

"We're going down Snake's Tongue." I try speaking through the stifling summer air blowing in our faces. "This is the best path in the whole town."

She squeals in delight once again as we hit a bump.

"Ride faster!" she demands.

"Are you going to tell your mom if we wipe out?" I ask almost out of breath as I pedal us up the hill.

"We're not going to wipe out," she says matter of factly. "I'm trusting you with my life, Diesel."

"I thought you didn't like nicknames?" I ask through heavy breaths.

"It's okay as long as I can give you one too."

"Then it's settled. You're Jersey girl and I'm Diesel."

"Agreed."

We reach the peak of the trail, and now it's time for the best part. The drop. I stop pedaling, and we begin to coast down the hill, gaining momentum with each passing second.

It feels like we're free falling, and even though I've been on this trail a million times before, it is ten times more fun with Jersey girl on the back of my bike. She hollers with glee our entire way down.

"Wheeeeee!"

As we freewheel farther down the path, I think all of all the places I'm going to show her this summer: the creek, the hideaway, my treehouse, the bigger football field on the other side of town.

We're going to have so much fun.

This is my kind of girl.

SECOND QUARTER

CHAPTER SEVEN

OLIVIA

S trings of stray pieces of maroon and white pom-pom plastic fly into my mouth as I sit in my usual spot on the stadium bleachers. I'm front and center in the middle of a sea of people dressed in all maroon and white, armed with plastic pom-poms, and cheering for the Bear Springs High School Chargers.

There's something deliciously addictive about the deafening roar of a crowd of rowdy football fans on a Friday night.

I simply love it.

This is a huge game for the school. We are playing one of our conference rivals and one of the best teams in the league. Sometimes I desperately wish I was one of the ones out there on the field, running with the ball, scoring for the crowd—but then I watch one of the players get flattened on the field by two big burly oafs and remember why I sit in the stands.

To stay alive.

"Hi, Olivia."

"Hey, Ginger."

I give her a curious look as she takes a seat beside me. Ginger and I are far from friends, so I'm not sure why she's sitting here and not with her usual clique.

"Our boy is looking great out there tonight isn't he?"

I snicker to myself. *Our boy?* Is she serious right now? Ginger is probably what you would call the high school hottie. She is a beautiful, popular, and for the most part, someone I can tolerate on most days, except for the fact that she occasionally talks to me in an attempt to get close to Mason.

"Catch it!" I blurt out as I suddenly stand with the crowd as it roars with celebratory cheers. The quarterback just threw Mason a Hail Mary pass down the field which he leaps up and catches in the corner of the end zone with barely his fingertips.

TOUCHDOWN!

In just the few short years that I've known my best friend, it's amazing just how much he's improved as an athlete. His body has always been big and strong for his age, but now it seems as if he can do the impossible with it, which I guess is why he is the most popular football player in our region. There's no doubt that he's going to go pro one day.

"Woo-hoo!" Ginger cheers. "He runs so fast doesn't he?"

With the ball still in his hands, Mason looks for me in the stands, and I give him one of our secret signs. I quickly throw up three numbers in rapid succession with my right hand. First the number four, then a three, then another four.

Mason then spikes the ball, raises his arms high, and does a little crisscross maneuver with his legs that both his teammates and the crowd eat up. They love it and begin to cheer for him even louder.

"Yeah, number eighty-eight!" Ginger yells.

I laugh to myself, because I just gave Mason the hand code for a very old touchdown celebratory dance that the two of us made up a few years ago in his backyard. I honestly didn't think he would remember it because I've made up at least seven different dances since then, but I should have known better. Mason never forgets. So now I owe him a burger and fries tomorrow. Since he's greedy, maybe two burgers.

"Oh my God, he was definitely looking at me just now!" Ginger exclaims.

I roll my eyes to myself.

"I didn't notice," I say plainly.

"You didn't see him looking in this direction?"

Yes—but not at you, idiot.

"All I saw was him dance in the end zone like a weenie," I joke.

"A weenie? No, girl, I thought his little dance was super hot. I'd love to show him just how hot I thought it was."

I pretend to shove a finger down my throat to demonstrate how grossed out I am by Ginger's words. She laughs for a moment, but then takes a lengthy judgmental look at me. My hair is in one big fuzzy ponytail on top of my head, my face is free of makeup, and I'm dressed in one of my many spirit wear outfits—baggy maroon sweatpants with the logo spelled on one side of the legs, and a matching oversized sweatshirt with our school logo front and center.

This is pretty much what I wear every day to school, and yes I know what she's thinking, but I don't care. I don't dress to impress anyone at school. I simply dress for comfort.

"I totally understand why you wouldn't see how hot Mason is. Boys aren't your thing, huh?"

Does she think I like girls just because I actually pay attention to football games and wear baggy clothes?

"What?"

"This is a judgment-free zone, Livy. You can be honest."

"Could you not call me that? I hate that nickname."

I clap loudly in support of the effort made on the last play. Mason tried to catch the last pass, but it was thrown too high.

"Good effort, Diesel."

"So listen, do you think you can put in a good word for me?" she asks. Finally getting to the point of this entire excruciating conversation. "With Mason I mean."

"Why can't you talk to him yourself?"

You seem to talk to so many other boys in school just fine.

"Obviously I could, but since you two are so close, I thought I'd ask you first. I mean you have the inside track. I was wondering if he ever talks about me? Maybe mention how pretty I am or something?"

I'm *actually* going to be sick this time. This conversation is literally poisoning me.

"Mason and I don't talk about who he likes or dates, Ginger."

"Aren't you two best friends?"

"He has a lot of friends. Why don't you ask one of the other ones?"

"Well, I guess I could talk to Pete or Simon about him."

I try my best to tune Ginger out because the opposing team's offense just took the field and our defense already looks tired. I yell out what I hope are some motivational side comments to them, because everyone knows that offense puts fans in the bleachers, but defense wins games.

"Come on defense!" I yell across the field standing straight up. "Get your head in the game!"

I take a seat and start nervously tapping my foot on the ground as I wait for another play. Our rivalry with the opposing team runs deep, and I very much want them to lose.

"Oh, you know what I wanted to tell you, Olivia?"

Is this pom-pom for brains still talking to me?

"Student council is looking for an events coordinator. Paula Simmons can't do it anymore, because she's failing English. Would you want the position?"

Ginger's question takes me off guard. I didn't imagine how quickly I would start to fall in love with Bear Springs when I first moved here years ago. In fact, sometimes I feel badly about it. Like I'm cheating on all of my old friends back in New Jersey. But the truth of it is, is that there is a love for football down here that my old school just didn't have. It's a deeply ingrained part of the culture here.

Game highlights are the topic of everyday conversation from kids to adults; because of that, I have slowly morphed from the kid who was the New Jersey transplant into a bona fide Bear Springs resident with incredible school spirit. In other words, a townie and a Georgia peach.

I wear our team colors all the time, I attend all spirit events, and becoming the events coordinator for the senior class would give me inner circle access to every school event—not to mention that it would be great for my college applications. It's certainly a tempting offer, but it's obvious that there are strings attached. Can I sell Mason out like that?

Hell yeah, I can.

"I'd be interested."

"Great! I'll put your name in as my personal

recommendation for the slot. You don't have to have to give a speech or anything, and we vote on Thursday."

"So soon?"

"Yep. If you're voted in then you start Monday morning. That's the day we have meetings unless something big is coming up like homecoming. Then we have meetings twice a week."

"Cool. Thanks, Ginger."

"No problem. Soooo are you going to see Mason after the game?

There it is—the string.

"He likes to look at film and stuff after the game so probably not."

"Oh well, whenever you get a chance to talk to him. Let me give you my number, so uh you can pass it along when you see him."

I hesitate for a moment. Something about this feels yucky. Mason and I never get involved in each other's love lives. Correction—if I had one, he wouldn't get involved. Not to mention that Mason doesn't do anything that he doesn't want to do. I don't even know if I can even fulfill my inferred part of this deal with the devil.

"Sure type it in here."

I hand her my phone.

"Awesome!"

The next thing I know, the clock has run out, and the opposing team takes a knee.

We lost.

Mason's going to be in a shitty mood.

MASON

"Give me three more."

"Three!" I exclaim while exhaling harshly.

"You can do it."

"I can't!" I grunt.

"You can and you will."

I'm in the varsity locker room, working on my upper body, and as usual, Olivia is my spotter. Sometimes I think that she loves football more than I do, and I feel badly that she can't play, so I make sure to include her in my training as much as I can. I always have. She's like my personal trainer, coach, and advisor rolled into one. There is no one else on this planet who wants me to succeed more than her.

"Just drop it on his chest, Olivia," Pete says as if he's totally amused. "That way he'll have to lift it."

"Shut up, Pete."

Olivia bends over and speaks to me directly in my face.

"Stop whining and give me two more reps."

"Your breath reeks," I tell her as I continue to strain to lift the barbell above my head. "Stop eating corn chips before we workout."

She purposely blows a long-winded puff of stinky corn chip breath over my face.

"You're just angry because you lost the bet."

"Maybe if you'd bench press heavier weight this week, you'll be able to reach a little farther for the ball when we play Madison High next week."

Suddenly I find a second wind, lift the barbell high, and then slam it back in its resting position.

"Are you serious right now?" I ask as I swiftly sit up and swing my legs around on the weight bench.

"It's not my fault that we lost the game. I'm killing myself out on that field every week."

Our quarterback, Sam Smith, overhears my comment and begins mocking me by pretending as if he's playing the violin.

"What!" I say standing to confront the entire room.

"You're breaking our hearts," Sam taunts.

"I did what I was supposed to do out there. The defense should have stopped the run."

I'm not usually the type to point fingers, but sometimes I do feel like I carry the entire game on my back and it's not fair. This is a team sport, not the Mason Bridgewater show. A statement that my father has been drilling into me ever since I made my first winning catch as a pee wee player and celebrated a little too long for his taste.

"Why don't you go bust the defense's balls for a little while, Olivia?" My longtime friend and teammate Simon says.

"Maybe I will have a word with Jackson and Spitz," she fires back with her hands sitting defiantly on her hips. "Those two looked more tired out there than my grandmom after cooking Thanksgiving dinner."

"Stay right where you are," I tell her.

Jackson has been drooling over Olivia for weeks now, and there's no way I'm going to permit anything to happen between one of my offensive linemen and my best friend. Football players (including myself) are all dogs, and all Jackson wants to do is to get into Olivia's panties. That would be a disaster.

Another one of my friends and teammates in the

training room, Pete, gives me a peculiar glance then asks Olivia a question in jest.

"You still making bets with Mason after all these years?" he asks her.

"I think he cheated." She pouts.

"How could I cheat?" I say. "You're just angry because you have to cook me a dinner fit for a king tonight."

"I thought we bet that I'd buy you a burger!" she challenges.

"A burger that you're going to cook with your own two little hands."

"Oh no I'm not!"

The room erupts in laughter.

"What kind of bet did you lose this time, Olivia?"

"It's a long story."

I lie back down on the bench, and quickly finish pressing my last three reps without even having her spot me. Truthfully I don't need Olivia or anyone to spot me. I just like to have her there.

"I'm ready to go to the market and pick up the groceries we need for my winner's dinner. Are you satisfied that I finished my set?"

"Eh, not really. Why don't you do an extra mile when you run tomorrow morning?"

Our team's number one defensive back, Jackson Kent, enters the training room. His eyes immediately home in on Olivia's ass and that's when I notice it. She's not wearing her usual baggy sweat suit ensemble. Today she's wearing a skin-tight pair of maroon leggings with a tank top and Charger hoodie that barely covers her butt.

Where the hell have I been?

Jersey girl's body is fucking hot.

"Why don't you go run with me?" I ask. Annoyed that Jackson is staring at her at all. "Those thighs of yours are looking a little chunky lately."

Then I slap the side of one of her legs.

"Mason!"

"Damn, dude, don't you know you're not supposed to talk about a lady's weight?"

"A lady?" I say incredulously.

I immediately regret the words as soon as they came out of my mouth. What I said was rude and embarrassing, especially in a room full of boys that she knows. Honestly, I don't know what came over me.

When I see the look of mortification on Olivia's face, I know that her wrath is soon coming. I quickly step behind her, grab her arms, and wrap them around her waist in a bear hold so that she won't hit me.

"Get off of me!" She struggles to get out of my grasp.

"No way. I can tell that you're fittin' to hit me."

"I sure as hell am. Just as soon as you get off me."

"Then I'm not letting go."

Jackson is standing across the room watching us. He isn't saying a word, but he doesn't have to. His body language is saying it all. He wants Olivia more than ever now.

"This is cheating!" she argues. "You're ten times my size."

"Ten times would make you super skinny and we both know that isn't—"

Umph!

Olivia lifts her foot and kicks her heel back into my shin with as much force as she can muster.

"Ow!" I scream through pain as well as raucous laughter. I can't help it. You have to love her spunk.

"You deserve worse."

I still don't let her go, because Jackson continues to watch. He may be more interested in her than ever now, but he has to know that JG (short for Jersey girl) belongs to me. Maybe not in a romantic way, but in all of the other ways that count. We're next door neighbors and best friends, and I'm not going to allow her to get hurt by some dude who just wants to fuck her. It's not happening. Plain and fucking simple.

"Are you guys going to just let him bully me?" she asks the room.

"We don't see anything," Sam says.

"Where is all this team unity when you're all out on the field? Why don't you throw the ball so he can catch it, Sam!"

Everyone laughs except Sam.

Even Jackson does.

"I swear that I'm going to kick your legs from under you if you don't let me go right this minute. You may never play ball again," she threatens me.

"Are you going to make me my dinner?"

I use one of my hands to start tickling her side, which isn't easy because I've got to still hold onto her with the other.

"I'm going to kill you, Mason!" she says in between fits of laughter.

"I want a vanilla shake too," I demand.

"I can't stand you. Oh my God, I can't breathe. I'm going to pass out."

Jackson takes a few steps forward as if he's going to do something to try and stop me. No one notices his subtle challenge but me, but I stare him right in his little beady eyes and then speak closely in Olivia's ear for his benefit.

"You're still talking, so you're still breathing."

"Okay, you win," she finally acquiesces. "I'll cook."

I stop tickling her, but I don't let go just yet.

"And?"

"And I'll make you a vanilla shake."

I smile at Jackson, kiss Olivia on the cheek, and then release her.

"Awesome."

Jackson mouths the word *asshole* to me, and I take some satisfaction out of the fact that I've made my point. Jersey girl is off limits.

"Why are you always terrorizing Olivia? I swear I don't understand why y'all are friends," Simon says to us shaking his head.

But our friendship is not for him or anyone else to understand.

It just is and always will be.

CHAPTER NINE

MASON

"Can I get some more fries?"

"How can you still be hungry? I made a ton of food."

"I'm a growing boy."

"I technically think you're finished growing."

"If there are no more fries, then I want my shake now. I'm still hungry and a bet is a bet."

Olivia rolls her eyes and in dramatic fashion pulls a half gallon of vanilla ice cream out of the freezer, grabs a spoon from the drawer, and plunks them both down in front of me.

"This will have to do."

She grabs a large orange for herself and sits across from me at the table.

"Where is your mom?" I ask.

"She went to some work thing."

After I shovel a couple of scoops of ice cream down my throat, my thoughts wander back to the game. No one likes losing, but I probably hate it more than the average player.

"So seriously, JG, what did you see when you watched the game? What do we need to work on?"

"Honestly, you were right. It's the defense. Jackson and Spitz probably need to lose a couple of pounds and ramp up their workouts. They get really tired fast."

"What do you think about Jackson?"

"I told you. He needs to lose a few," she says nonchalantly as she continues to peel her orange.

I grab it and finish peeling it for her.

"Other than football I mean."

"Like in what way?"

"Would you date him?"

"Date him?"

"Here." I give her back the peeled orange.

Her initial reaction to my question satisfies me. It doesn't seem as if she's interested in Jackson at all, so I don't think I have anything to worry about.

"Thanks."

We stare awkwardly at each other for a moment.

"What's up with you?" she finally asks. "It was

just one game. Why are you being all sensitive about it?"

"I'm sorry about what I said in the gym today."

"Which thing that you said?"

I look down in shame.

"All of them."

She continues to break her orange apart and eat it.

"You were playing around, weren't you?"

"Of course."

"Well, then I'm fine. I'm just one of the guys, right? You should be able to joke around with me like you do with them. You're only apologizing because I'm a girl. If I were a dude, I'd be right in that room with y'all all the time anyway—playing ball and kidding around."

"True."

"So, umm, since we're asking questions. What do you think about Ginger Hampton?"

"Ginger?"

"Yeah."

"Why are you asking me about Ginger Hampton?"

"Just wondering if she's your type of girl."

I cock my head to the side wondering where she is going with this line of questioning.

"Ginger is everyone's type of girl."

"So you'd be interested in her?"

"I'm not sure. I feel like this is a friendship test, and I'm nervous about whether I'll pass or fail. Did she do something to you? You want me to get somebody to kick her ass?"

"No, nutball, I can fight my own battles. I'm asking because she wanted me to give you her phone number."

I grin.

"Ohhh, she did?"

"Yeah."

"So give it to me then."

I wipe a little bit of juice dripping down Olivia's chin with a clean napkin. I may be the greedy one, but she's always been the messy one.

"So ... you want it?"

"Yeah."

"You're going to call her?"

"That's what you do with a phone number, Einstein."

"Okay, umm, I'll text it to you."

I watch as Olivia nervously forwards me the number. I can't exactly read her odd body language, but I'm not going to look a gift horse in the mouth. Ginger Hampton's nickname behind closed doors is

Ginger Snap. Supposedly she has so much control over her pussy that it feels like she can clamp down and *snap* your dick in two. Who wouldn't be curious about that?

"About earlier—" she says.

"What about earlier?"

"The stuff about Jackson."

My face tightens.

"Yeah, what about him?"

"I was caught off guard when you asked me earlier, but I guess you already know that he asked me to The Harvest Dance."

That fucking dance is in six weeks! No one is asking anyone to the dance yet.

"When did he ask you?" I try plastering on a fake smile.

"I thought you knew."

"When did he ask you?" I ask again through gritted teeth.

"The first week of school."

I'm going to kick his ass.

"And what did you say?"

"I said I'd think about it."

I swallow another large spoonful of ice cream. It enables me to think before I speak, because I'm really about to say something dumb right now.

"But you hate dances."

"That's not true. I make 'em up for you to do in the end zone all the time."

"Okay, but you hate dances that require a date."

"Who says I do?"

"You've *never* brought a date to any of our dances."

"Things change, and I'm a senior now. I don't want to have any regrets. For once I want to be like every other girl."

"But you're not like every other girl. That's what makes you different."

"It's what I want."

"Are you going to wear a dress?" I ask incredulously. Olivia never dresses up. It's not her style. She's Sporty Spice, not Posh Spice.

"Yes, douchebag, I'm going to wear a dress. I've worn dresses before."

"To church."

"Why are we debating this again?"

"I'm just going to be honest here."

"Please do."

"I don't want you taking anyone from the team to the dance."

"Why? What's wrong with me?"

"Nothing."

She's getting me all wrong. It's not that she's not good enough, it's that none of them are.

"I don't tell you who to date."

"You might as well have," I say.

"What's that supposed to mean?"

"Tell the truth. You didn't want to give me Ginger's number tonight, did you?"

Olivia shifts in her seat looking uncomfortable. It's not her personality to do things that she doesn't want to do, not unless it's her mom asking, so I'm curious to know how Ginger convinced her to pass along her number.

"I didn't want you to get a venereal disease before the age of eighteen."

"And I don't want you dating anyone I play with."

"That's not even the same thing. You're comparing apples to oranges."

"What if Jackson does something to you?"

"Like what?" she scoffs. "I've known him just as long as I've known you. What would he do?"

I stand up and start pacing the kitchen floor.

"You're so naïve sometimes, Olivia. He can *do* a lot of shit. I can't believe you're from New Jersey."

"The last time I was in New Jersey I was eleven years old, and I lived in the suburbs, not the hood.

Look, you're being ridiculous. All the guys I know in this town play on our football team. What do you want me to do? Date someone from the next town over?"

"Let's change the subject," I say because I don't know how to answer her without sounding selfish.

"I'm supposed to be helping you with environmental science tonight. You need at least a B on the test if you're going to bring your grade up."

She stands in front of me slack-jawed.

"Oh my God. You're not kidding. You really don't want me dating Jackson."

"You'd be putting me in a fucked up position if you do, because if something happens to you and I have to make a choice, it will always be you, Olivia. Always you."

CHAPTER TEN

I'm five minutes early to the last student council meeting before the Harvest Festival, so I take a moment to enjoy the quiet. I'm sitting in the student lounge, sipping on a bottle of peach tea, and wondering how it is that I'd never been in this room once until this year.

Mason and I haven't really talked about Ginger and Jackson after the spirited conversation we had in my kitchen, but I can only assume by my present circumstances that he must have called Ginger and is making her very happy. Any icky feelings I had about my part in making that happen are over. They both seem quite okay with the arrangement. She's bouncing around the hallways happy as a clam, and I even caught the two of them whispering with each other under the stairwell toward the gym.

"Hi, girl." Ginger takes a seat next to me at the small round table I'm sitting at.

"Hey, Ginger."

"Where is everyone?"

"I don't know. I'm the first one here."

"I guess they're running behind. I think most of them are coming from the west side of the building. I'm glad it's just the two of us though, because I wanted to bend your ear for a minute."

What else is new?

"So ... has Mason said anything about me lately?"

"Nope."

"Nothing at all?"

She looks as if her feelings are hurt.

"Sorry, I told you that we don't really talk about each other's love lives like that."

"Then what *do* the two of you talk about?" she asks in a huff.

"Sports and stuff like that."

"Oh, right ... since he probably didn't tell you, I wanted to let you know that he's taking me to the homecoming dance and I have you to thank for it."

I don't know why I'm surprised but I kind of am. Mason goes to the dance every year, but after the conversation we had, I thought ... I don't know what I thought.

"Congratulations."

"Yeah, right? I will be going with the most popular football player in the state."

Is that all she cares about?

"Yep."

"So how about you?"

"What about me?"

"Who's going to be your date? You've done all this work in such a short time on the council to make the festival ten times better than it's ever been."

"Really?"

"Your ideas are bomb-ass, girl! Setting up food stations along the hayride trail was brilliant, and asking alumni for donations to pay for the mini fireworks show was genius."

"Thanks, Ginger." Aw, maybe she isn't so bad. "But I think I'd just rather work the night of the dance. Make sure things run smoothly."

"All there is to do is organize refreshments beforehand and pay the deejay. There's nothing else for you to do the night of, but dance, and I've got the perfect date for you."

"Date?"

The other students we were waiting for start entering the room, but Ginger keeps talking.

"He's totally interested too. I snuck a picture of you the other day and showed it to him."

"What?"

Total invasion of my privacy.

"Don't worry, this is what I do. I've hooked up a lot of my friends. Haven't I, Mary?"

"She definitely has."

"And get this— he loves the sporty types like you *and* he's in college!"

"College?"

"Yeah he goes to Georgia Union, so he's local."

"I'm sorry, Ginger, but why would a boy in college want to go to a high school dance?"

"Because it's Scott Dobson."

I'm speechless. Scott was the quarterback and captain of the football team back when I was a sophomore. He's a legend at the school. Tall, dark, gorgeous, and a bit of a badass. Me going to The Harvest Festival Dance with the infamous Scott Dobson? What on earth would a guy like that see in me?

"And he's my cousin."

"I don't think I ever knew that."

She claps her hands with excitement.

"We could get dressed together. Have Mason and Scott pick us up at my house. Take pictures. It will be like a double date. Don't worry, I'm going to help you with your hair and your makeup and we'll find you a dress. You can't wear school sweats to the dance."

The girls at the table giggle at her jab. Ginger is so good at manipulation that I think she just simultaneously slapped and hugged me.

"Wait, I—"

"Trust me, Livy, we're going to have the time of our lives."

CHAPTER ELEVEN

Everything about Ginger's house is exactly what I thought it would be—brand new construction, that sits on a piece of land that I swear is as big as one of the local playgrounds.

The house has been decorated for the season. In almost every room there are seasonal decorations such as pumpkins that light up, dried, colorful corn cobs, and strings of gold and orange lights everywhere.

Outside is a beautiful rock and flower garden in the yard which features a man-made babbling brook, Koi pond, and seasonal flowers such as mums and pansies everywhere.

Her family is definitely Georgia rich, which is a not-so-quite creative description that my mom came up for families in our area with "new money." There is even a room the size of my bedroom dedicated to hair and makeup, and after Ginger is finished blowing out and curling my hair and applying my makeup, it's time for me to slip on the dress that I purchased online.

It fits perfectly.

It's a simple blush-colored mini dress with spaghetti straps, that even I have to admit almost transforms me into one of those impeccably dressed girls you see online.

"Damn, girl, you look like a million bucks when you clean up!" Ginger exclaims. She's basically patting her own self on the back for my makeover, which maybe she has the right to do since it was all of her own handiwork, but she doesn't have to say it in such a condescending way.

"Thanks, I think."

I turn around and look at myself from various angles in the mirror. Between the loose curls in my hair, the sparkly pink lip that pops against the color of my skin, and the way my dress slides over my curves—I feel beautiful. Really beautiful for maybe the first time in my life.

I take a quick selfie to send to my mom hoping that

it will smooth things over between us. I think she was a little hurt that I didn't get dressed for the dance at home, seeing as how I've never gone with a date before. Yet she didn't say anything to me about it, probably because she's so happy that I'm going at all and that someone like Ginger is my friend—which is kind of a stretch to say. What's more accurate to say is that Ginger and I are in the middle of a mutually beneficial relationship.

Ginger's mom pops her head inside the bedroom. She's a petite woman who wears way too much makeup and jeans so tight that I think she may lose consciousness at any moment.

"Oh, you both look so beautiful. I can't wait for the pictures. Your daddy's got the camera ready, and, Ginger darling, your date is here."

"Thanks, Mama."

On our way down, Ginger checks her makeup for a final time, which has been impeccably applied but then at the last minute stops to pull open one of her dresser drawers.

"Clean underwear just in case." She raises her eyebrows up and down mischievously.

My stomach rolls over because she is obviously planning on having sex with Mason if they haven't already. Although I'm not really sure why, the thought of it makes me ill, and I'm sure it shows all over my face.

"Are you a virgin, Olivia?"

"I'm sorry—what?"

"Have you had sex?"

"That's kind of a personal question, Ginger."

"You're right it is, but I was just asking in case you're worried about my cousin. He's in college and everything, but don't worry, he's not expecting you to do anything with him tonight."

"That's good then, because I wasn't planning on doing it with him ever."

She grins.

"Oh, so you are a virgin, because I've never not heard any girl say that they plan to sleep with my cousin."

"He's quite popular at Union I take it?"

"It's ten times worse than high school. Everyone knows him there."

"Of course, half of our high school goes to Union."

"Well, that's true."

I turn my back on Ginger and look at myself in the mirror, more nervous than I was already about this night. Questioning why I've agreed to this date. I should have just stayed in my lane and worked the event like I planned. What am I trying to prove by going to the dance with one of the most popular guys to have ever attended Bear Springs Senior High?

"Girls!" Ginger's mom sternly calls for us again.

"Coming!"

Ginger descends the staircase first to find Mason waiting at the bottom dressed handsomely in a slate gray pair of slacks and suit jacket with a crisp white T-shirt to dress them down. It's not like I've never seen Mason dressed like this before, but tonight seems different.

Tonight, I'm seeing what half of the female student body sees in him. I've always known he was funny, talented, smart and loyal, but tonight he seems taller, sexier, and more adult than I've ever seen him.

He smiles brightly as Ginger makes her way down the steps, but his smile soon turns to a stupefied gaze as soon as he recognizes that it's me behind her.

"Do you like my dress?" she asks Mason, assuming that her appearance must be the reason why he's stunned and speechless.

"Um yeah," he says actively trying to clear his throat. "You look nice."

"Do you like how your bestie looks? I did her

makeover as a surprise. I can't wait to see the looks on everyone's faces. I'm not saying I did it all myself, but I basically did it all myself."

She mockingly brushes off one of her shoulders with her hand.

"You look really pretty, Olivia." His eyes assess my entire ensemble from head to toe. "Really pretty."

My stomach flip-flops.

"Thank you, D."

An awkward silence sits heavily between the three of us. I don't know what Mason and Ginger are thinking, but in this moment I feel like something has shifted between Mason and me, but I'm not exactly sure what it is.

I just know that it frightens the hell out of me.

CHAPTER TWELVE

MASON

I know it's rude as hell, because I'm in the middle of Ginger snap's living room, but I can't keep my eyes off of Olivia.

The dress she's wearing tonight is short and tight and it looks like I'm going to be fighting half of the damn football team off of her. I don't know whether I'm incensed or impressed with her.

"Did you pick that dress?" I whisper in her ear while Ginger is distracted talking to her father.

"Yes, why?"

"It's too short."

She punches me in the arm and laughs.

"What are you my paw-paw now?"

"I'm not kidding, JG."

"What is wrong with you?"

"Your cousin is pulling up in the driveway," Ginger's mother announces excitedly. "Could you guys brave the cool weather for a few moments and take photos in the garden?"

What the hell? Ginger didn't mention anything about a cousin coming over. I can only assume that her family takes school dances seriously and are coming by the house to take pictures as if I'm taking her to the damn prom.

"Who's that?" I walk over and ask Ginger.

"It's my cousin. You know him. He was on the team a few years ago. Scott Dobson."

Holy shit.

Scott Dobson is her cousin?

"Why is he here?"

"He's Olivia's date. You didn't think she was going to the dance by herself did you?"

It all begins to unravel completely in front of my eyes. Scott walks in the door in all his confident, cocky, pain in the ass glory and makes a beeline directly for Olivia. The second he reaches for her hand, my entire body clenches with rage.

"You must be Olivia," Scott says to her. "You look amazing. I'm Scott Dobson."

"I know who you are," she says grinning stupidly.

"Ready to turn this party out?" He offers her the crook of his arm.

"Sure," she says almost meekly.

When has Olivia ever been fucking meek?

I am seething.

We take a few painful pictures outside in the cold, and then we all head to the dance in the same car. Riding together was my idea, so I'm driving. There's no way I'm taking my eyes off of Scott and Olivia for one second. He had a bad reputation as a whore in high school, and I can't imagine that it's gotten any better in college. I just have to get her through this night untouched, and then I'll make sure that they never speak again.

"You're originally from New Jersey, right?" he asks Olivia.

"Yeah, how did you know?"

"I definitely remember you from school."

I watch the two of them through the rearview mirror of my truck. When Olivia lowers her head, and a small smile spreads across her face, my entire body begins to grow taut.

He's such a liar. Can't she see through this good guy ruse of his? Doesn't she remember all the stories she heard about him back in the day? Where is my tough as nails best friend at? She's disappeared underneath the pink dress and lipstick.

"I'm surprised to see you tonight, man," I say to him. Interrupting their little love fest back there. "You're a big college dude now."

"I like to visit from time to time. Homesick and all that."

Union is thirty minutes away. How is he homesick?

"Just didn't think you would do the high school dance thing again."

"I missed a couple of 'em when I was in school because I got into trouble a few times. I wasn't allowed to attend." He laughs. "Imagine that. The team's captain not allowed to go to The Harvest Dance when the damn thing kicks off entire homecoming week."

"Oh yeah, now I remember. It was because of a drug thing right?"

That wipes the smile clear off of Scott's face. He starts to shift uncomfortably in his seat and cuts his eyes at me.

"Weed," he says in an attempt to clarify the type of drug he was caught with, as if it matters.

"Right ... well Olivia doesn't smoke, so no fun for you tonight I guess."

"Mason!" Ginger admonishes me. She leans over and whispers in my ear. "You're being an asshole."

I clench the steering wheel tightly when Scott grabs one of Olivia's hands and starts playing with each of her slender fingers. He's not the idiot that I remember in the locker room years ago. He totally understands what I'm doing right now, and he's passive-aggressively challenging me to "bring it."

"No worries, Bridgewater, that was the old me. You do a lot of growing up in college. You figure out who you are and what you want. You make smarter decisions. I don't need pot when there are so many other ways to entertain myself."

He grins at me in the mirror and then turns to Olivia.

"Your nails look nice. Did you just get them done?"

She smiles goofily again and nods yes.

What. The. Fuck.

If we don't get out of this car relatively soon, I may swerve us all into a ditch.

"We're here!" Ginger exclaims. "The lights outside look great, don't they? Wait until you see everything that Olivia did for the midnight hayride."

When Scott gets out of the back, he holds the door open and extends his hand to help Olivia out of my dad's truck, as if he's a gentleman. It's so fake. That's not who he is at all. Never has been and never will be.

"Milady," he badly jokes using an old English accent as he offers her his arm again.

Since Olivia is not used to wearing tight short dresses like the one she has on, she has a difficult time maneuvering herself out of the car. It hikes up as she scoots herself across the seat and out the car, so of course, Scott can't help but step in as her official dress smoother. An obvious attempt to touch her hips and ass.

"Let me help with you that."

This is totally it I think to myself.

There's no way Olivia is going to let him get away with that. He smoothed the back of her dress twice with the palm of his hand. It was so unnecessary and totally gratuitous. I saw her chase down and wrestle Simon to the ground for five minutes for playfully slapping her butt one time when we were fourteen years old, so she's definitely not going to let that slide.

Except she does.

"Thank you."

Thank you?

I must be in the fucking twilight zone.

~

"Is the punch spiked?" I ask Ginger as soon as we enter the gym.

"We just got here."

"And I want a drink."

"It's not spiked, but I stashed a flask in the locker room when we were all decorating."

"Get it."

"Okay. Wait here," she says sounding a little disappointed in me.

We haven't been inside the party for more than five minutes before Scott and Olivia start dancing. It's like he couldn't wait to get his greedy hands all over her. I know I'm being a prick to Ginger, but I'm out of my mind with jealousy and contempt.

It's like a light switch turned on inside of my head.

I should be the one holding Olivia. It's her senior year and her first official date to a dance. It should be me by her side not him.

There's not even a slow song playing, and he is holding her by the waist as they seductively dance together. I stand directly behind him so that she can see me. We know each other better than anyone in the world, and I know that this isn't who she is. She doesn't like guys like Scott Dobson. If she likes anyone it's unattainable guys like the nerds from her favorite boy band, Thunder Road, not handsy, pot smoking, quarterbacks in college.

I hold her gaze with a murderous look as her hips continue to rock back and forth to the music. Delighted that I'm making her feel uncomfortable. She whispers something in Scott's ear, and he walks off toward the refreshment table. Then she approaches me.

"What are you doing?"

"What do you mean?" I say icily.

"You're totally freaking me out. Are you trying to ruin my night?"

"Yesssss," I hiss.

"Why, Mason?"

A tear starts to roll down her cheek and I realize that I'm handling this all wrong. I'm not angry with her. I'm angry at myself.

I step in closer to her. Cradling the side of her face with my hand. Brushing the one lone tear away with my thumb.

"Because you should be spending it with me."

"I don't understand."

"Do you trust me, Jersey girl?"

"With my life," she whispers.

I stare deeply into her eyes and in this moment it's as if everything around us has faded into the background. There is no music. No people. No Ginger or Scott. There's only us.

Mason and Olivia.

And the only thing between us now is years of friendship and a pretty pink dress.

I lean over and place my mouth on hers, pulling her into my body with the hand I have now wrapped around the base of her neck. Her lips arc soft. Her mouth warm. I slide my tongue inside of hers and begin exploring her mouth gently. She is unsure of herself and doesn't quite know what to do with her tongue which makes the kiss all the more sweet.

I am her first.

I can tell.

When we finally come up for air I am breathing heavily and so is she and I tell her.

"I think you do now."

THIRD QUARTER

Freshman Year

"I wanted to meet with you, Mr. Bridgewater, because I've personally reviewed the results of your placement testing and thought we should discuss them."

I am in the office of the head of the biology department of Georgia Union University, home of the fighting Pythons, and where both Olivia and I attend college. Upon graduation from high school, I had a lot of enticing offers on the table for places to attend school to play football, but most of them were from Ivy League universities that Olivia didn't have a chance in hell of getting into—so those were definitely out. I didn't tell her that, of course, because she would have had my head on a platter if she knew, but there was no way I could be apart from her for four years.

"What did you want to discuss, Dr. Hammond?"

"At first, when I saw that a major player of our football team was also majoring in biology, I was skeptical. I haven't run into too many players with your high level of academic aptitude or interest in biology."

"I think you're buying into the stereotypes of the dumb athlete, sir," I say curtly.

"I'm sorry if that's what you think I'm saying. It's just that my experience tells me that most student-athletes have focused all of their energies on their athleticism and not on academics. You're a pleasant surprise is all I'm saying, and I think you should seriously consider a profession in the sciences."

"Thank you for the kind words, but I'm a football player first and foremost. I'll always have my education to fall back on when I can't play anymore."

"So your degree from Union is your backup plan?"

"Exactly."

"I wouldn't be so sure about that. The sciences are a competitive area of study too. Internships are hard to come by, and it isn't easy to get into good postgraduate programs, so I'd take it a little more seriously."

"I'll consider what you've said. Thank you for the meeting."

Dr. Hammond sighs with dissatisfaction. He obviously didn't get the response he was hoping to receive from me.

"Okay, Mason. I hope you give it some thought. Football is a brutal way to make a living. I'm just saying that you have something that a lot of other students on your team don't have—options."

Dr. Hammond has given me a lot to think about, and unfortunately has stirred up doubts in me that I've long had concerning choosing football over a career in the sciences. My mom has always encouraged my interest in the medical field, whereas, my dad has always encouraged my talent at football. I'm sure they didn't mean to confuse me, but they have done just that. Sometimes I'm not sure if my interest in either one is genuinely mine or just a result of parental encouragement.

As I make my way across campus to meet Olivia, I receive an incoming call from an unknown number on my cell phone.

"Hello?"

"Dude!"

It's my uncle and pseudo sports agent, Uncle Quincy. Every time he calls it's from a different number which is why I didn't know it was him at first. He's a gambler, a lawyer, and my dad's younger brother. In fact, we're only twelve years apart which is why I call him by his first name. He would kill himself if I called him uncle anything.

"Where are you, Quincy?"

"I'm in Vegas at the Bellagio. You've got to see it one day. It's just like the movies. Dude, what are you doing right now?"

"Meeting my girl."

"What else is new?"

"I'm not in the mood for it, Quincy."

"I'm just saying, Olivia is a sweet girl and all, but is she really worth you playing ball at a second-rate college?"

"Union is not a second-rate school."

"And why are you always meeting her every day? You should give that girl some breathing room. She needs to find her own way in this world too."

"She's my best friend. Of course, we hang out all the time. You wouldn't be saying this if this were a guy."

"You kiss all your best friends on the mouth?"

"How is this any of your business?"

"You're suffocating her, dude, not to mention yourself. Have you even tasted any of that Georgia Union tail since you got there?"

"I've literally been here three weeks and the answer to your question is no. Olivia is my girl. My heart. I would never cheat on her."

"We'll see if you're singing the same tune when girls start camping out at your dorm after you win a game or two for that sorry university."

"A wonderful university where my dad, *your brother*, makes a living."

"Which is fine, but you and I both know you could have been playing for Michigan, Notre Dame, or Stanford. You would have gotten TV time and a great education."

"Scouts come to Union all the time."

"Only if they have a reason to come, which is in fact why I called you."

"Finally the point of this call. What is it?"

"I have it on good authority that a few select scouts are going to be visiting Union, upon my request, to watch you play the home game against Tech U. If you give them a little showtime in that game, I guarantee that you will be in a great position to enter the draft."

"Freshman year?"

"Kids are entering the draft early now these days, especially phenoms like you, and you've been on these guys' radar for years. So you talk to that quarterback of yours and make sure he throws you the ball during that game."

"I'm a freshman."

"But you're a starter."

"Nobody is going to throw me the ball because I ask them to."

Especially the asshole quarterback, Scott Dobson. He's been hazing me since I got here. My only reprieve has been the time that I spend with my father in the training room.

"My brother knows everybody on the team. They won't listen to him?"

"I'm not going to ask Dad to talk to the players for me? That's a bitch move. They would never pass me the ball again."

"Fine." He sounds angry. "I'm out here busting my hump to get you set up in the sweetest way possible, but if you want to blow it because of formalities then—"

I forgot that I'm dealing with a crazy person. My dad has always taught me to just tell Uncle Quincy whatever he wants to hear and things will be much easier.

"Don't worry about it, Q. I'll handle it. Just play twenty dollars on red seventeen for me at the roulette table."

"Gotcha, dude! I'll call you when it gets closer to game time."

"Thanks again."

"No thanks are necessary between family, superstar. Just make sure you're in tip-top shape for the game. Talk to you later."

"Bye."

OLIVIA

Practically every day since we've started Georgia Union, Mason meets me on the yard when my afternoon class ends at two o'clock. His schedule is quite full, and the two of us take classes at completely opposite ends of the campus, so it's generally the only time we can spend together.

When he comes within eyesight of me, he stops walking, holds his arms out wide and waits with a huge grin on his face. He's waiting for me to run, jump into his arms, and wrap my legs around his waist.

As if.

It's never going to happen, but Mason already knows that, because it's actually a private joke between us. In one of my favorite Thunder Road videos, the lead singer has a scene where he does the same thing with the main video girl. The only difference is he's singing to her while she runs toward him.

"When are you going to stop embarrassing yourself with that whole act?" I tease.

"When you finally break down and do it."

"It's never going to happen." I laugh.

"If I was the lead singer of Thunder Road it would happen."

"Abso-fucking-lutely."

"I'll give you a head start for saying that shit and that's about it."

"You better not—"

"Three ... two ..."

I don't wait to hear the rest of the countdown before I start running. I was always a fast runner, and with a head start I could have had a chance to make it to my dorm before Mason, but my boyfriend is an athletic phenomenon. It doesn't take long for him to catch up to me, lift me up in his arms, and run with me like I'm a sack of potatoes.

Everyone who's walking to their next class or just hanging out on campus watches the spectacle we're making of ourselves and starts laughing or cheering us on. A year ago something like this would have made me feel embarrassed, but now I'm starting to get used to it. I have no choice. Even as a freshman, everywhere that Mason goes on this campus he is recognized. Football is everything to the students here. Plus, half of our town attends Union.

"Put me down."

"That doesn't even sound sincere."

"Oh, I'm serious."

Mason puts me on my feet and quickly kisses me.

"How was class?"

"The same."

"It will get better."

"I just didn't think I'd be taking all of these remedial courses."

"They're not remedial."

"Well, how come you don't have to take any of them then?"

"Stop comparing yourself to me or anyone else. You are Olivia Robertson and you are one of the most interesting and unique girls I have ever met. You will figure out what your major should be eventually and even if you don't, I will always take care of you."

"Oh, because you're going to be the superstar wide receiver in the NFL."

I wrap my arms around his neck.

"That's right and it may happen even sooner than you think."

I recognize the glint in Mason's eyes. There clearly is something he hasn't told me.

"What do you mean by that?"

I step back from him and take a seat on the grass. Patting a spot beside me.

"Sit."

"My uncle is in Las Vegas."

"Is he?" I smile.

Mason's Uncle Quincy is a colorful character who acts informally as his agent and protects his interests. A plan created by Mason's dad so that he'd always have people around him who he could trust.

"Gambling as usual."

"I assumed that was what he's doing. What else is there to do in Vegas?"

"Get married."

"Yuck, I would never want a Vegas wedding. Too tacky. Too over-the-top."

Mason rolls me over on my side.

"So what kind of wedding would you want?"

"I want a church wedding, in the summer, by the water, and I want a Thunder Road cover band performing at the reception."

"You are insane and very particular."

"You asked me, and that's what I want."

"I am not having some tired-ass boy band rejects perform at our wedding."

"Who says it's *our* wedding?"

Mason playfully starts to growl and tickle me again. We roll around on the freshly mowed grass and I continue to laugh as blades of grass end up in my mouth and damn near up my nose.

"I can't breathe!" I exclaim. "Stop it."

Mason rolls over and ends up on top of me. The weight of his body is heavy and hot and turns me on even in the middle of a campus full of people. My desire for him grows stronger with each day we're together and is probably fueled more by the unknown.

I am still a virgin.

"If you're still talking, then you're still breathing."

He kisses my mouth swiftly.

"Get a room!" someone walking by jokes.

Mason rolls back over on the grass and clasps his hands behind his head.

"I need to win this game against Tech U, babe. I need Dobson to throw me the ball."

"You're just a freshman."

"Who is a starter."

"He doesn't trust you yet. You have to give him time."

"And I'm sure stealing his date in the middle of Harvest Dance didn't help matters."

"That was eons ago."

"That's funny because he acts like it was yesterday."

"They're just hazing you because you're new and because your father works here. They don't want you to think you're special."

He turns and stares right in my face. "When I so clearly am."

"You've always thought too highly of yourself."

"So have you."

"You must be high. I couldn't stand you when we first met. I thought you were an annoying, oversized, blowhard."

"But you got on my bike."

"That broken down mountain bike."

"That bike was a work of art."

"Do you still have that thing?"

"My mom stole it in the middle of the night like a thief thanks to your mom."

"Yeah, my mom loves a good yard sale."

"At least some little boy somewhere will be able

to say he's riding Mason Bridgewater's bike one day. He might even be bragging about it right now."

I roll my eyes and sigh.

He's hopeless.

And so damn adorable.

"Or a little girl is."

"It's a boy's bike, babe."

"Bikes don't have a gender."

"We're debating this again?"

"Gender is a social construct created by man."

"I thought you were past this. If you want to play football then there are amateur women's football leagues, Olivia. They've even got those lingerie ones. You would look fucking hot running down the field in a red bra and panties."

I hit him in the side with my fist.

"*Oomph!*"

"There should be professional leagues in the states for women just like there are for men."

"I'm not disagreeing with you, but the problem is that part of the reason why men like to watch football is because it's a violent sport. The closest thing to war without having to really go to war. No man wants to watch a woman get her ribs fractured or her teeth knocked out, and they definitely don't want to pay to watch it."

"Whatever." I suck my teeth.

We've had this debate a million times over the years.

"Listen, I know you love football, probably more than any guy or girl I know, but there are plenty of ways to love it and to be a part of it without having to play it."

"I'll remember this speech when the time comes for you to retire."

"Now that's just plain ole mean, JG."

Humph.

"You didn't finish telling me why this Tech U game is so important to you."

He presses his lips together like he's holding onto the words. Like he doesn't want to tell me.

"Spill it." I prod him further.

"Quincy has some scouts coming to the game."

"Scouts this early?"

"He said that one of them might make me a decent offer if I enter this year's draft."

The thought makes me nauseous.

"The draft?"

CHAPTER FIFTEEN

I sit up to full attention on my knees.

"You are *not* entering the draft, Mason Bridgewater."

"Shhh," he reprimands me. Still casually lying on the ground like he didn't just drop a bomb on me. "Someone will hear you."

There are eyes and ears everywhere on campus especially when it comes to athletes, so this probably isn't a conversation we should be having here on the yard, but he started this so I'm going to finish it.

"Mason," I whisper. "You've been in college for like two seconds. You are not entering the damn draft."

"Guys are entering the draft earlier and earlier. You know that it's a big risk playing college ball for four years. What if I get hurt and I never get to go pro?"

"That's not going to happen."

"I appreciate the confidence, babe, but it's not realistic to say that. This is a gladiator sport, and at some point, I will get hurt. The question is when and how badly. I'd rather it not be in college. I'd rather it be after I've secured a decent pro contract for myself, and given you the wedding you want and built us the house that we'll need for all of our kids."

"Kids?"

Mason laughs at me. He knows that I'm not frightened of much, but the thought of a human being coming out of my body is simply terrifying.

"Lots of 'em."

"I don't have babies with idiots."

"You don't have babies at all unless you have sex."

He wiggles his eyebrows suggestively.

"We've had this conversation," I say defensively.

The truth is that I've been thinking about having sex with Mason a lot lately. It's hard not to. He's drop dead gorgeous, charismatic, sexy, and more importantly, I know that he cares about me. More than probably any guy ever will.

He's also on the fast track to becoming football

famous, and I know that there are girls everywhere on this campus that are more than willing and able to sleep with him. Do I want to have sex with him for the right reasons? Is it because I'm afraid that someone else will do it if I don't, or is it because I truly love him?

"Take a chill pill, tough girl. I'm only kidding. I'm perfectly fine with you setting the tempo. I will wait for you for as long as it takes. Except for a kiss though. I want one right now, and I won't wait for it."

He growls as he grabs me effortlessly by the hips and pulls me on top of him, but I press my lips tightly together to avoid the kiss in protest of his considering the draft.

"Nope."

"Why not?"

"Not until you reconsider the whole draft thing."

He stares earnestly into my eyes and just like that, everyone around us seems to fade into the background.

I only see him.

Hear him.

"I'm not making any definite decisions right now, because you're right. I just got here, and there's no reason to rush things, Okay?"

I didn't realize how tightly wound my body was

from just the thought of Mason entering the draft. Immediately his words give me a sense of relief.

"Okay."

"You trust me, JG?"

"With my life."

After a brief but passionate kiss, we decide to grab lunch at the campus grill called The End Zone. We've been eating here over the last week or so, because we like it better than the cafeteria food. We both order the grilled chicken sandwich combo, and then start to go over homework while sitting at a booth in the corner.

I pull out my calendar to show Mason what my assignments are for the week. Sometimes I wonder if I made it into Georgia Union on my own merit or simply because my mother works for the university. School can sometimes feel overwhelming at times.

"Okay, you should start working on this English paper tonight. If you just do an hour a night, you'll get it done three days ahead of time. That way I'll be able to edit it before you need to turn it in."

"I don't need you checking my homework, *Mom*," I say facetiously. "I just need a little help getting organized."

"Okay but—"

Two girls stop at our table and interrupt us

specifically to speak to Mason. Scratch that. I mean flirt with him.

"Good luck on the Tech U game, Diesel. You're looking good out there."

"Yeah, we'll be cheering for you, D."

I glare at them for a moment like they've both lost their ever-lovin' minds.

"Do you not see me sitting here?" I ask them both.

"What?"

One of them responds with a totally fake California Valley girl accent, and the other doesn't respond at all as they both turn to walk away with satisfied grins across their faces.

"I said—" I grow louder and angrier in response, but Mason quiets me with a hand on my thigh.

"Chill, babe."

"Did you not just see that?"

"They were just football fans."

"They were Diesel fans."

"That's a good thing, right?"

"Not when they disrespect your girlfriend."

"You're being emotional. How are they supposed to know that you're my girlfriend?"

"They called you by the nickname that *I* gave you!"

"Babe, in fairness, you know that everyone calls me that now. You should be proud. You gave me a name that followed me all the way from middle school to college. There will never be a time that somebody calls me by the name Diesel and I don't think of you."

"Wonderful," I deadpan.

"I love it when my Jersey girl gets jealous. It's such a turn on. Now come over here on this side of the booth and sit next to me."

"You're too damn big. We'll be all squished together in the seat."

A devilish grin appears on his face.

"That's exactly the point."

Sophomore Year

"Have a seat, Olivia."

I take a seat in my advisor's office after receiving an email from him requesting a meeting.

"So, I asked you to meet with me today because I see that you are only partially registered for spring semester. All I see in the system is that you're enrolled in your two remaining prerequisites. I'm assuming the reason why is because you haven't declared a major yet."

"That about sums things up, Mr. Killum."

"Just out of curiosity have you talked to your mother about your options?"

"I don't think that my mom can help me figure out what to do with the rest of my life. Only I can do that."

"True, but she knows this university well. She could help point you in the right direction, consider all the possibilities, and perhaps pick the right professors."

"If it's all the same to you, I'd rather not involve her."

"All right, so let's talk. What did you see yourself doing when you chose to enroll in Georgia Union?"

"I have no idea. I was undeclared when I made the decision to go here."

"Why did you choose this university?"

"I agreed to go to Union because the tuition is free since my mom works here."

"Is that the only reason?"

"Yep."

"That's a perfectly valid reason. College is expensive. Tell me, what did you dream about doing or becoming when you were a little girl?"

"Playing football."

"Really?" he responds as if he's stunned. As if it's the wildest thing he's ever heard.

"Yes, *really*. I played it all the time as a kid, and I stupidly thought that one day I'd play it as an adult."

"You mean professionally play?"

"Yes, I told you it was stupid."

"I don't think it's stupid at all. In fact, I think it was a reasonable assumption to make. No one dreamed when I was a kid that women would have their own professional basketball league, and now look. It's a reasonable assumption to think that it would happen with football too."

"Basketball and football are very different though. I didn't at first, but now I realize and have accepted that people just aren't ready to watch women play football yet, but it doesn't change the fact that I still love the sport."

"As millions of other people do in this country, but actually, Olivia, you've given me a great deal of information to help you. I've taken a look at your original application to the university, your involvement in student council, and the classes you've taken here so far. Couple all of that with the fact that you love football, and I think I have a good idea of what direction to point you in.

"I think you could have a future in a variety of areas: publicity, event planning, marketing, or promotions. You could combine your love of football and any of these majors. Ball clubs have or hire publicists, event planners, and marketing teams all the time."

Something inside of me smiles. Mr. Killum just gave me something that I so desperately needed … direction.

"And so you're saying there are jobs like that in the NFL?"

"Of course. It's a billion-dollar company that is always trying to promote itself. This will keep you involved in the sport you love and making a good living while doing so. In fact, both collegiate and pro leagues have a need for all types of marketing and promotions support, and Union has a good track record of helping our graduates find full-time employment in those fields."

"You've given me a lot to think about, Mr. Killum. I appreciate it."

"I'm happy to help, but, Olivia, you should probably think quickly about next semester. Classes fill up fast. Maybe consider discussing what we talked about with your mom so she can help."

Maybe I'll stop by her office.

"I'll be back first thing Monday morning to register, Mr. Killum."

"Excellent. See you then."

My mother is what you would call a modern superwoman. She is fiercely determined, extremely talented, and pretty much successful at everything she tries—except for her marriage to the man who should have been my father.

She works in the music department of the university where she teaches jazz voice. While I love my mother and deeply admire her for her talent, as well as for her strength in raising me alone, we couldn't be more different.

My mom is quite feminine, loves pastel colors, flowy dresses, and floral perfumes. She's also very beautiful, somewhat traditional, totally creative, as well as talented, organized, and polite.

I, on the other hand, am very different. I'm a tomboy, nontraditional, uncreative, disorganized, love the color brown, prefer sweats, would rather wear a *clean* scent, am not considered a beauty by any stretch, and I can't sing a single note.

It's difficult being so different from the woman that gave you life. I struggle to see myself in her all the time, and it may explain why I've struggled with figuring out my place in the world. Who I am, what I'm good at, and what the right path for me is.

Maybe that's why I'm so attracted, yet so totally envious of Mason. He knows his place in the world. He knows that he's a ballplayer and that he'll be a ballplayer for a long time, and when that's over he knows that he has the intelligence to be anything else that he wants. A doctor, a lawyer, or whatever.

There has to be peace in that sort of knowledge. Peace that I envy.

I peek into my mom's office which is open because this is her time for office hours. She is sitting at her desk typing something on her computer. I tap gingerly on the doorframe.

"Mom?"

Her eyes pop up, and when she sees that it's me, she smiles warmly.

"Hey, sweetie, this is a pleasant surprise."

"Yeah, I just came from my counselor's office, and since I was nearby, I thought I'd stop in to say hello."

"How are classes? Are you having a good semester so far?"

"Yes, classes are fine. I was meeting with Mr. Killum to discuss next semester because I haven't registered yet."

"You really need to register or they'll give away

your dorm room, Olivia. You don't want to commute do you?"

I sigh to myself.

I love my mother dearly, but she always finds a fault or a way to fix anything I'm doing.

"Don't worry about it, Mom, I'm handling it."

"Good. So how's Mason doing? Are you two still hanging out?"

"He's doing well. Having a great season so far."

"Yeah, the Chargers have never looked better since he joined the team. We were lucky to get him."

"Yep."

"Tell him to call his mother a little more often. You two are only thirty minutes away, but it seems like three hundred miles to us because you don't live at home anymore. A call once in a while would be nice."

"I'll tell him."

I stand up to leave.

"This was a very nice and unexpected visit, Olivia. It's weird that I don't see you much and I work here. Thanks for dropping by. It was good to lay eyes on you."

"It was good seeing you too, Mom."

I give my mother a brief hug and a kiss on the cheek and then head back to my dorm. I decided not to talk to her about selecting a major, because it's always been difficult for me to talk to my mom about anything serious. We're not friends. I'm her daughter. Plus, it just didn't seem the right time to bring it up.

I'll talk to Mason instead.

CHAPTER SEVENTEEN

I'm surprised when I see the infamous Scott Dobson sitting on a bench in front of Hamilton Towers (my dorm building) and talking on his phone. There are several reasons for my surprise. One is that I've never seen him at this dorm before. Ever. The other is that I know the team has practice right now. So why is he here?

Then I see the reason why.

Shit.

His entire leg is wrapped in a soft brace from ankle to crotch.

"Hey, gorgeous."

"What on earth happened to you?"

"Motorcycle accident."

"Ooh, and you have a black eye too. Are you sure you didn't get on the wrong side of someone's fist?"

He chuckles.

"No, just the wrong side of a large buck in the road. I swerved to get out of the damn thing's way and ended up like this."

"A deer and a motorcycle, huh? You were lucky that a broken leg and a bruised face are all you have."

"Ain't that the truth."

"So why are you in front of my dorm? You should be sitting somewhere with that leg propped up watching Netflix."

"I would if there was someone available to take care of me."

Scott is a charmer and a flatterer. I experienced a little of it firsthand when he took me to The Harvest Dance back in high school, and I see it once in a while when I come to the games. He always makes it a point to say hello and flirt a little. I think he does it primarily just to get on Mason's nerves.

"You're so full of it, Dobson."

"Are you still with Diesel?"

I turn my lips up in a half smirk. Scott knows full well that the two of us are together, because how could you not? Mason likes to make a show of it.

"Yes, Scott."

"Doesn't hurt to ask."

I change the subject.

"Coach doesn't make you go to practice even with a broken leg?"

"It's not broken. I tore a few ligaments and yes he does require me to come to practice, but I ain't going. I've been playing football every single day for most of my life. Today I just want to lie like broccoli and talk to the prettiest girl in Hamilton Towers."

I can see the pain in Scott's eyes when he talks about football. I think this injury is much more of a big deal than he's letting on. Maybe he feels like it's career ending.

"Your leg will get better, Scott," I say as I finally sit down next to him.

He pauses for a moment then smiles at me.

"You didn't ask me why I was on the motorcycle."

"Huh?"

"I'm the quarterback of the team. I wasn't supposed to be on a motorcycle. It's dangerous. We even sign a code of conduct contract that specifies that we're not supposed to participate in any activities that could cause us bodily harm. Motorcycle riding is on that list of banned activities."

As it should be.

"So ask me," he says.

"Ok, why were you riding? You've got Virginia U coming up and now you won't be able to play in one of the biggest games of the season."

"Graham will do a good job. I taught him everything I know."

Graham is the backup quarterback.

"That's not really the point, Scott. I don't get it. Why would you risk everything you've worked so hard for?"

"I've always been careful about everything for the sake of football. All my decisions have been for the sake of football. What I eat. The games I could play. The summer camps I could go to as a kid. The friends I could have. It's all been about the game and I was tired. For once I wanted to make a decision that was all about what I wanted."

Scott hangs his head and I pat the knee of his uninjured leg gently as a small gesture of comfort. I've never been in his shoes, but I think I can empathize with Scott's pain. I've always dwelled on how not being able to play football was so unfair to me, but I never put much thought into how much these guys sacrifice to play the game.

"I never thought of it that way before and you're right. You should be able to have a little fun without having to always consider how it will affect football. I hope you figure things out. You're a good player, but you're also a great person who deserves great things."

"Can I marry you?"

We both start laughing.

"I'm promised to another."

"Yeah, and he never lets me forget it. All jokes aside, I appreciate you not calling me an idiot for this." He points to his leg.

"Of course not. You're Scott motherfucking Dobson. You'll never be an idiot."

"Aw, that was sweet. Say, Olivia, have you been to one of our frat parties yet?"

"Uh-uh."

"You're a freakin' sophomore and you haven't been to a Theta party yet? You need to come tonight as my guest. Bring some of your girls."

"I don't know." I hesitate.

"You can bring your boyfriend if you want to, although I don't know anyone who brings their boyfriend to a frat party."

"I'll ask him."

"He'll probably be there anyway. He goes to plenty of parties without you and he'll probably be at this one."

That sort of irks me, but I realize that it's my own

fault. I often tell Mason to go on without me a lot, because parties aren't my thing unless I'm helping to plan them. I don't like making small talk with airheaded sorority girls all night while he socializes with his teammates and their groupies.

But maybe I need to second guess that way of thinking.

Maybe I'm making choices that aren't in my best interest either.

"I'll think about it. There are a couple of girls on my floor that might want to go."

Kira will definitely want to hang.

"Awesome. I'll tell the door to look out for you. Come find me when you get in. I'll be the dude standing on crutches or sitting in the middle of the room in a recliner."

"I'll see you later then."

CHAPTER EIGHTEEN

The guys on the team are in low spirits after hearing the news about Dobson. He's a senior, our star player, and the big Virginia game is coming up. I, on the other hand, might be the only one who's not depressed about it.

I'm pissed.

It was totally selfish of that egomaniac to get on a motorcycle when he is so important to the team. His decision to do that speaks to his character, or lack thereof.

I had plans on spending the evening with Olivia tonight, maybe take her to a movie or something, but I think I need to hang with the guys and help our backup quarterback, Graham, feel more connected to the team. Once we get our off-the-field chemistry right, it will be much easier to get the game day chemistry right.

Many of the players on the team are in the same fraternity. Theta is popular with athletes and tends to attract a lot of ballers, although I didn't pledge it. I went with one of the more academic fraternities on campus and they were glad to have me.

The Theta frat house is wild during party season. When we arrive, there are kids everywhere. Inside, outside, in the yard out back and on the roof deck. The music is on full blast, and the bass from the hip-hop playing is practically making the walls shiver with every beat. The women are dressed in their party best, short dresses or tight jeans, and they all have a drink in their hands.

I'm the designated *party ambassador* for the guys tonight which means that it is my job to get them drunk, get them laid, and drive them home if necessary since I'll be sober. I'm at the makeshift bar grabbing a few drinks for Graham when I notice Olivia walk through the door with three other girls from her dorm. She didn't tell me she was coming tonight which is strange, but I don't care about that as soon as I take a look at her. I mean *really* look at her.

She looks amazing tonight.

Blue balls amazing.

She's wearing a pair of tight jeans with a few purposeful rips in the front, a simple cream colored camisole top that pushes her breasts up high in a way that makes me want to lick in between them.

She sees me standing at the bar and smiles. I smile in return until I see Dobson hobble his way over to her on his crutches. I might be imagining this shit, but they greet each other as if she's his guest.

What. The. Hell.

"Diesel, you said you needed three drafts and three vodka shots?"

"Yeah," I respond totally distracted.

"Okay put your drink donation in the jar and I'll get you the shots. You want Stoli or Grey Goose?"

All of the girls that Olivia are with are fawning over Dobson. Rubbing his shoulders and asking him about his leg, but it seems as if he's only paying attention to one of them and that's my girl.

"Stoli's fine."

Olivia swears that Dobson taking her to the dance a few years ago was a pity date that Ginger arranged, but I knew the minute he laid eyes on her that it wasn't as simple as that. I believed him when he told her that he already knew who she was. Who wouldn't? Olivia is the kind of girl that's hard to forget, not to mention that she's drop dead gorgeous —especially because she doesn't have a clue that she is.

"Your girl is looking especially hot tonight. Surprised to see her at a frat party. Usually, you keep her locked up in her dorm."

"I don't keep her locked up anywhere, jackass."

"Never seen her at a frat party though."

"She's been to a few at my frat."

"It kind of makes me believe what I heard today."

Simon is goading me. Over the years the guys have relentlessly teased me about my relationship with Olivia. They all really like her, but it's just what guys do. I've allowed it because I don't care what they say about us.

No one makes me smile or laugh like her.

No one has my back like her.

No one turns me on like her.

"You're waiting for me to ask aren't you?"

"Did she tell you she was coming tonight?"

"No."

"Is she talking to you right now or to Dobson?"

"Get to the fucking point, Simon."

"She was seen in front of the towers sitting with

Dobson, talking to him, touching him. They were supposedly real cozy."

"Give me another shot please."

I throw back one of the vodka shots in my hand that goes straight to the head, and then I drink another that the bartender hands me.

"Give these to Graham," I say to Simon.

"Aren't you the designated driver tonight?" he asks.

"Not anymore."

I practically stomp like a child over to where Olivia and Scott are standing. Vodka mixed with fury are quickly traveling through my bloodstream and emboldening me.

"You didn't say you were coming tonight," I say in an almost accusatory way to Olivia.

"Hello to you too, Bridgewater," Dobson greets me sarcastically with a Cheshire grin across his face.

"I wasn't talking to you."

"Let me talk to you for a minute outside," Olivia requests as she grabs my arm.

She smells just as good as she looks.

"Instead of worrying about if she got your permission to go to a party, how about you telling her how gorgeous she looks tonight."

He wants me to hit him.

"Scott, quit it," Olivia says.

The fact that she is even addressing him makes me irate. Doesn't she see how disrespectful he is being to me? To us?

"What the fuck is your problem, Dobson? You think this is a game?" I step in his face. "You can have any girl in this room, so why the hell are you after what's mine?"

"She isn't your property."

"She's mine."

I grab Olivia by the waist and pull her into me.

"Mason!"

Before he even tries it, I warn him.

"If you even move one of those crutches toward her, I will knock you out right in the middle of your frat house. I'm sick of this shit. I don't care if you're the captain of the team. I don't care about any of that. Leave Olivia alone or you'll be hobbling on both of those legs tonight."

Olivia pushes me with all the force she can muster out of the room and into the next one.

"I'll be back in a minute," she tells her girlfriends.

Once we're in the dining room section of the house I allow Olivia to rip me a new one. I knew it was coming anyway.

"Why are you acting like a crazy person? Are you drunk?"

"I had two measly shots."

"Do two shots make you drunk?"

"I'm not drunk, JG. I'm furious!"

"Why? Because I'm here?"

"No! Why does everyone keep talking to me like I'm keeping you locked up in a prison somewhere? I don't care that you're out tonight with your girlfriends. I *want* you to go out and have fun. What I don't want is that jerk sniffing behind you everywhere I turn and you going for it."

"You're being ridiculous."

"Was he at your dorm today?"

Her face drops.

"I mean yes but—"

"To see you?"

"Not exactly."

"What does that mean?"

"It means, that I never got around to asking him who he was there to see."

"That long of a conversation huh?"

"Mason—"

"Did he invite you to this party?"

"Yes, and I didn't mention it when we spoke, because I didn't think you were going to be here."

"What does that have to do with anything? You thinking that I wasn't going to be here. I thought we told each other everything?"

"We do."

"We obviously don't."

"Listen, you're clearly a little tipsy and not yourself. I'm out with my friends, and I'm here to have a good time, not argue with you. For some reason you allow Scott to get to you when our relationship is perfectly harmless. He's just messing with you sometimes, and you fall for it every single time."

She just doesn't get it.

"So this is my fault?"

"Tonight it is."

"Then by all means. Party your ass off. I'm out."

I storm out of the room and see Dobson pushed up on another girl in the corner. This is all a game to him. How he treats football. How he treats women.

So I punch him.

Dead smack in his eye.

"You're a dick," I tell him.

And then I keep walking out the door and all the way home. By the time I arrive, I'm freezing and the vodka has worn completely off. I'm cold, and angry, and feel a little sorry for myself. At the beginning of this day, all I wanted to do was spend some time with my girl, not hang with the guys or punch Dobson in the middle of the frat house.

How did my evening disintegrate into this?

Now I am all alone.

CHAPTER NINETEEN

OLIVIA

I am still staring in the direction of the front door of the house that Mason just exited through wondering what just happened. He's gone, Scott is holding his eye in pain, and everyone's staring at me.

I came to this party with my friends to try something different. To be more social. If I'm going to promote a ball club or a living, I better learn how to be a better party girl. So that's why I've come to have a good time.

Part of me wants to follow Mason to his dorm and figure out why he just hit Scott like that, but another part of me realizes that he was acting like a total kid. Storming out of the frat house like a bratty kid who has never been told the word no.

"Are you ok, Scott?"

"I'm cool, gorgeous. I just have a matching set of black eyes now."

His eye is looking more purple by the minute.

"Scott, I know what Mason did was wrong but why do you continually push his buttons like that? He's not a freshman anymore, but you act like you're still hazing him as if he is one. He's your teammate. Your equal. In fact, he's one of your best players."

Several party goers have surrounded us to shamelessly listen to our exchange. I'm not trying to embarrass Scott any further, but I can't let this slide. No matter how ridiculous he may act, I will always have Mason's back.

"He shouldn't have talked to you that way," Scott replies.

"Maybe he shouldn't have, but that's for me to worry about and for me to handle. It's none of your business."

Scott stops smiling.

"I don't treat Mr. Sensitive any differently than any of the other guys on the team. It's just so easy to get under his skin."

"I don't understand what pleasure you get out of that. Mason's never done anything to you, but I'm asking you to stop. If the two of us are going to remain friends, I'm asking you to stop."

"What's everybody looking at?" he angrily barks at the crowd. "Go away and get drunk. This is a party."

Scott doesn't respond to my request. In fact, he doesn't finish talking to me at all. Instead he summons two girls over who flank both sides of him and then hobbles back over to his recliner.

I, on the other hand, just stand there looking stupid until my friend Kira comes over with a drink in her hand.

"This is for you. It's a vodka and cranberry juice. I think you need it."

I take the glass and take a long sip. I don't normally drink alcohol, but this is sweet and almost refreshing, so I take another sip.

"Thanks."

"I can't believe you had two hot football players fighting over you tonight."

"They weren't fighting over me at all. It was a dick swinging contest and nothing more."

"Thanks for that visual. Do you know whose dick is bigger?"

"Kira!"

"I'm kidding," she chuckles. "Listen, it might have been a whole whose dick is bigger thing for Scott Dobson, but I saw the look in Diesel's eyes.

That dude looked genuinely distraught. Like he lost his best friend or something."

"But he didn't lose his best friend. I've been right here the entire time."

"Then maybe you need to be wherever he is right now to remind him of that."

CHAPTER TWENTY

OLIVIA

My friends are troopers and decide amongst themselves that if one of us leaves the party then we're all going to leave. Even though it's against regulations, we all take a to-go drink with us as we walk in the cold across campus back to Hamilton Towers.

We will pass Mason's dorm before we get to Hamilton, so I'm thinking carefully about what I'm going to say when I see him. I reconsider all of my actions up to this point and wonder if I did something to contribute to how the night ended.

I don't know who's in the right or the wrong at this point. All I know, is that I need to talk to him. I hope he's here. It takes me five freezing minutes to finally make the decision to ring Mason's doorbell, and when I do his suite mate answers the door.

"Hey, Olivia."

"Hi, is Diesel here?"

"I think he's asleep."

"Oh–" I say quickly. "I'll talk to him tomorrow then."

I'm almost out of the door when I hear a door crack open and then his voice.

"Wait."

I turn to find Mason standing in the doorway with nothing but a Georgia Union towel wrapped around his waist, and his hair dripping water from a fresh shower.

"Come inside."

I walk silently inside of his room and sit on the edge of the bed completely tongue tied by his smooth muscular body. It's a feast for the eyes to watch as each muscle ripples and contracts with every small movement that he makes.

He doesn't bother to get dressed, and he doesn't say a word. He just sits down on the chair at his desk opposite me and stares at me from head to toe with angry green eyes.

His fury rattles me.

And excites me.

I cross my legs to stop the dull ache that is growing in between them, and then I try pulling up my top so that my cleavage is covered because suddenly I feel underdressed.

"Did you wear that outfit for him?" he finally asks with displeasure.

"That's an absurd question."

"What's the fucking answer?"

"I don't wear clothes for anyone but myself, and stop using that language."

"You don't wear anything special for me?"

He stands up in a powerful stance.

"No, I can't say that I have."

"Then maybe that's the fucking problem."

He starts walking over to the bed.

"Maybe you're not clear on what we are to each other."

"I'm very clear," I say swallowing the lump forming in my throat.

He stands directly in front of me, spreads my legs open, and kneels in between them. Magically his towel stays put and doesn't fall to the floor. I'm nervous that it will.

"We're not childhood pals riding our bikes together down near the creek, and we're not high school buddies sharing burgers and lifting weights. All of that shit is in the past. It is our past."

"I know that, Mason."

"You mean much more to me than our history, Olivia. I loved you at eleven, I love you at twenty, and I will always fucking love you. So when I see you giving anyone, especially that douchebag Dobson, the impression that they come between us– then that's when I have to step in and bring some order to this shit."

"Mason–"

"You belong to me, Olivia. Call it sexist, call it patriarchal, call it whatever the fuck you want to call it, but just recognize the truth. You are mine. So act like it."

I take both of my hands and cradle his face in between them. I bend my head and kiss him on the lips. The kiss is gentle at first, loving, and then it grows more intense.

He takes his huge hands and uses them to easily slide me forward on the bed. Then he begins kneading my hips as his head falls in between my breasts. He peppers each one of my them with kisses, and I can feel the warmth of his breath through the fabric of my top.

I grow immediately wet in between my legs. My

panties are so drenched that I'm afraid it I will soak right through to my jeans.

"I smell you," he growls.

He stretches my cami down on one side and one of my heavy breasts pops free. He sucks on the nipple with great ferocity as he plays and pinches the nipple of the other.

Mason and I have been intimate like this many times before, but never with this degree of want between us. I don't know if it's the vodka coursing through my veins or because emotions ran high tonight, but I want him more than I ever have.

I am ready.

I slide my hands through his wet, slick hair and start to moan from the pleasure he is continuing to give me. He growls in response. Loving how I run my hands through his hair when I'm turned on.

"Take off your top," he orders.

I yank my cami up and over my head, releasing my breasts, and offering them up to Mason.

"You are so beautiful, Olivia. It wrecks me when Scott looks at you like he know what's underneath your clothes."

"He doesn't know." I pant

"I know that. I know you. I just...sometimes I can't help but feel the way that I do."

"Then try harder to help it, because you're pissing me off."

Mason smirks devilishly then licks the corner of his mouth.

"I'm going to to taste you now."

CHAPTER TWENTY-ONE

OLIVIA

"First, we're going to peel off these skin tight jeans you have on. They make your ass look great, but it's time for them to say goodbye."

Mason stands and then pulls me up to stand as well. My eyes are fixated on the bulge poking through his towel as I fiddle with the zipper of my jeans.

"Here." He grins after noticing that I'm gawking at his huge appendage. "Let me help you with that."

Mason does most of the work to shimmy off my jeans, and once they're off, he tosses them clear across the room with a hungry look in his eyes.

"Lie down on the bed."

I obey.

He stares at me with wonder as I lie sprawled out

on top of his dark blue comforter feeling more beautiful by the minute.

"Black lace panties look so hot on you."

He starts to rub against his bulge with the heel of his hand. The way he is looking at me makes me feel powerful.

"Maybe I wore them for you," I tease.

In seconds, Mason kneels back down on the floor, slides his hands underneath my ass, and pulls me forward. I yelp in surprise from the sudden movement.

"Eeek!"

Mason slides the crotch of my panties over to one side and begins to lick in between my legs making sure to pay special attention to my clit. He devours me so deliciously I don't know what to do with myself. My body just reactively responds and my hips start to move and my hands grip his scalp.

"That's it, baby," he encourages me on. "Give me this pussy. It belongs to me."

An angsty, winding ache begins to build inside of me. I'm going to come, and when I do, it's going to be powerful. My hips continue to move and my breathing grows more shallow and rapid.

"It's hot in here," I complain. "I'm sweating to death."

Mason lifts his head up.

"I'm going to finger fuck you now."

"You're killing me," I say almost breathlessly.

He slides one of his oversized fingers inside of me.

"Good, that makes two of us."

He continues to move his finger in and out of me while at the same time checking my facial expressions the entire time.

"You look like you want to come right now," he says in an unrecognizable bass heavy voice.

"I do," I pant.

"But you've been bad tonight. You don't deserve to come."

"Mason," I plead softly.

Then he slides a second finger inside of me and continues to stroke them inside of me as he places his mouth back on my pussy. I feel full, and freaky, and I begin muttering incomprehensible strings of sentences as he takes a strong suck of my clit.

Then I start moaning loudly.

Thrashing my head about.

It feels that damn good.

"Shh," he warns. "Do you want Ben to hear you coming for me?"

"No."

"That's right. This a private matter between the two of us. So you need to be quiet while I remind you who this pussy belongs to."

Oh my God.

Everything that Mason says gets dirtier by the minute and turns me on by the second.

His fingers are coated with my desire.

My fingers are clenching the covers.

I am panting like I just ran a race.

I'm going to explode very soon.

Mason stops eating me out and then pulls his fingers completely out of me.

"When we make love, Olivia, you're going to wind and lift your hips like you just did except you're going to lift them a little higher for me. You understand?"

"Yes."

"Lift them now and show me you understand completely."

I lift my hips slightly off the bed and he pats me softly in between the legs with the pads of his fingers. It feels nice.

"Higher," he demands again.

Then he slaps me again between my legs. A little harder this time. The vibration of the slap feels surprisingly good, and I moan in pleasure.

"Higher, Olivia!" he commands with a stern voice.

The anticipation is driving me crazy, so I raise them really high this time and he whacks my pussy with an open hand and with more force than before. It rocks my entire core, and I scream in pleasure as a sudden gush of wetness falls between the lips of my sex. He follows it with another quick slap and then massages my clit with his thumb and I'm right at the edge of the cliff, but not completely over it.

"Please," I beg him to end this.

"Please, what?"

"I want you inside of me."

"I don't care what you want."

"I need you."

"Does your pussy ache?"

"Yes."

"Does it ache for me?"

"Yes!"

"Good, because I ache for you all of the time. Every fucking day. I want you so badly."

"I want you too."

He starts to suck on my breasts again.

"Fuck, I love your tits."

Then he slides his hand between my legs again. Slipping one of his thick fingers back inside of me.

"You are so wet, Olivia."

"I know."

He continues to stroke inside of me and I can tell that he is slowing things down. Maybe contemplating what to do next. He wants to be careful with me. That's why I love him.

"Do you trust me, Olivia?"

"With my life," I whisper.

He slides his tongue inside of my mouth and kisses me ravenously. I can taste the saltiness of my need mixed with a faint hint of vodka on his tongue and it turns me on even further.

"Now, Mason."

I've always known that Mason has a huge dick. It's part of the reason why I've been hesitant to have sex with him. I didn't see how there'd be any way that he would fit inside of me, but lucky for me, the human body has the amazing capacity to stretch.

He lines up the tip of his dick toward my entrance and begins to slowly push inside of me with great precision. He's so worried about my comfort, it's sweet.

"I'm sorry, baby, does this hurt?"

"No," I lie.

It definitely doesn't tickle.

"I want you so much. I've been dreaming about this night. About you."

"Me too."

"You're so fucking tight."

I squeeze my eyelids as he continues to try to break through my barrier, but once he gets through something changes.

It starts to feel really good.

"When you're ready, baby," he pants, "Do what I showed you."

After a few more strokes inside me, I begin to catch Mason's rhythm and lift my hips when he thrusts forward. The sensation of when we both meet each other's strokes almost sucks the air out of me.

I feel full.

And wanton.

And sexy.

"That's it, JG," he groans. "I knew it would feel like this. Damn, I'm so lucky."

I'm practically clawing at Mason's back at this point. The orgasm is building inside of me at a rapid pace because of all of the foreplay beforehand. And the next thing I know it sneaks up on me.

"Mason!" I scream in orgasmic release.

Forgetting that Ben is literally ten steps away from the room.

"Fuck!" he exclaims in a guttural way. "This pussy is going to kill me."

Mason lifts one of my legs over his shoulders and starts to pound me hard from the side and I come again.

"I think I'm coming again!" I cry.

Mason's response is incoherent to me at this point. All I see are fire bursts inside of my head, and all I hear is a faint ringing in my ears.

I am spent.

My hair is a sweaty mess.

My cheeks are flushed.

My pussy is throbbing in the best way possible.

The two of us are both lying side by side, coming down off of our orgasmic highs, when he grabs something from under the sheets.

"I think I killed your panties."

I'm not sure when it happened but my lace panties are ripped to shreds and are balled up strips of fabric in his fist.

"Do you think Ben left before we, uh, finished?" I ask a bit embarrassed by what he possibly heard.

"That's what you want to talk about right now?"

"Do you think he heard me?"

"I think the entire campus heard you." Mason laughs. "My girl is a screamer. I love that shit."

"Oh my God."

Mason cracks up with laughter.

"So what if he heard? I was giving it to you good, babe. You couldn't help but be loud."

Unbelievable.

He's even cocky in bed.

"Let's make a bet," I challenge.

"What kind of bet?"

"I'll bet you that I won't make a peep during round two or I cook you breakfast."

"Round two?" Mason licks his lips. "You sure you want to take that bet? I'm going to give it to you doggy style next."

"I'm positive."

"Then it's a bet!"

CHAPTER TWENTY-TWO

Junior year

I have one of the best seats in the house, but I'm sitting in a huge college stadium in Alabama which means that Mason can't see me. This stadium is five times bigger than ours, thanks to the generous donations of their boosters, but that doesn't make them a better football team. My guy is kicking ass and the Pythons are giving Alabama a run for their money this fine Saturday morning.

The only good thing to come out of Scott tearing his ligaments last year is that the backup quarterback, Graham Beckton, stepped up in a major way and has been feeding Mason the ball every single game. Their chemistry is phenomenal and has put our team in the position to be a serious contender for the national championship.

The halftime show starts when someone fills the two empty seats in front of me. I'm surprised to see that it's Mason's uncle and another man with him. He doesn't notice me at first, and before I can say hello, I overhear a bit of their conversation.

"Since we have a personal relationship, John, I have no problem sharing with you that Mason has been getting a few interest offers in the last few weeks. You and I both know that he belongs on a major stage like Seattle or Dallas. I'm hoping that Arizona has an equally enticing offer."

"So he's definitely entering the draft? I heard that his parents want him to earn his degree first."

"Trust me, my brother wants Mason playing in the league by summer. He can finish college later."

"He looks great today. Let me go back and talk to my front office and see what we can work out. I've got to go catch a plane, so I need to leave now."

"Cool, we'll talk later."

After the scout leaves, I address Quincy. He's totally out of line holding that meeting. Mason's told me stories about how he operates, and there's no way that he knew anything about that little meeting his uncle just had on his behalf.

"Hi, Quincy."

"Oh, hi Olivia. I didn't see you there."

"I see that."

"You're looking kind of good these days."

"Was that supposed to be some sort of a compliment? *Kind of?*"

"Of course it was. You were a little tomboyish back in the day, I'm just saying it's nice to see you embracing your feminine side. The curly hair is a nice touch."

I roll my eyes.

"Thanks."

"Diesel's doing good I see."

"Yep, he caught two touchdowns already."

"Sweet."

"So, Quincy, does Mason know you're here?"

"Nah, I didn't get a chance to call him before I landed. This is a pop-up visit."

"To meet with a scout."

"Yeah, so?" His nostrils flare.

"I know you are his family, and I don't mean any disrespect, but I don't think you have the authority to arrange interest deals for Mason."

"I can't have my nephew going into the draft

without some assurances. There's nothing worse than when the television camera pans on a player who is waiting to get drafted and he never gets picked. It's embarrassing."

"But who says that Mason is entering the draft?"

"I say so."

"You?"

"He should have done it a long time ago, but he was too busy looking out for everyone else but himself."

"What do you mean by that? I think his folks just want him to get his degree first."

Mason's uncle gets up and moves directly in front of me.

"I know you're not as naïve as you pretend to be. I'm not talking about my brother and his wife. I'm talking about you. *You* are the only reason why my nephew is still in Georgia, playing on the small stage, for a two-bit university."

I grow defensive.

"You wanted him to go pro his freshman year. It was too soon. Football is full of grown men who are itching to hurt receivers. It was in his best interest to wait a while."

"Listen to yourself. You think that you know

what's best for Mason. You think you know better than his own family? You don't, little girl."

"I didn't know you were so strongly against our relationship."

"I just wish my nephew could make decisions based on what he wants and not what you need."

That hurts.

"Are you saying that he isn't his own man?"

"I'm saying that he's so worried about what you are going to say and how you're going to feel that he puts his entire life on hold, so that he can support your fragile ego."

Now that effin' stings.

"Why are you talking to me like this, Quincy? Where is this hate coming from?"

"Don't misunderstand my frankness. I don't hate you. I just think it's time that someone tell you the real deal. You're a nice girl, Olivia, and you should be with a nice boy from Bear Springs who wants to get a job, get married, and go to ball games every season. But Mason is destined for more, much bigger things, and he hasn't quite tapped into his full potential yet."

He continues his lecture.

"We missed out on a lot of money these last two years because he refused to enter the draft, but I won't sit back anymore and just let him make these bad career decisions for some tail."

"I didn't put a gun to Mason's head. If he didn't enter the draft it was his own decision. You're giving me way too much credit."

"This isn't just about the draft. He was making dumb decisions over you even earlier than that. You do realize that he could have gone to a dozen better colleges than Union, right? He got offers from Stanford and Michigan just to name a few."

I didn't really know that. Mason acted like Union gave him the best offer because he was a hometown kid. Maybe that was all a lie?

"He picked Union because the tuition is free for kids of full-time staff. He didn't want to carry heavy student loan debt."

Quincy scoffs.

"You really don't get it, do you? Mason had a ton of free ride offers to play football. He wouldn't have paid for school no matter where he went. He went to Union because it's the only school that you could get into."

My heart feels like it's shattering into tiny pieces and stabbing me in my throat. I don't want to listen to what Mason's uncle is saying, but I believe every painful word.

I am a liability.

"You want my advice? If you really love that boy like you think you do, you'd break up with him now and save him the trouble of breaking your heart later. Like they say, if it's meant to be it will be."

I've run my drills for a third time, before I check my cell phone again. I'm waiting for a text or call back from Olivia, but there's nothing. As one of the football program's new publicity interns, I expected to see her more, but it's quite the opposite.

I never see her.

If I didn't know better, I'd think that she was avoiding me, but I do know better and Olivia would never do that. She's a straight shooter. A tough cookie. She would tell me if there's something wrong. Our relationship promise to each other has always been a hundred percent honesty or bust.

I cut out of practice fifteen minutes early to go look for her. She's not in her dorm, class, the cafeteria, or on the yard, so I try The End Zone. I spot one of her old suitemates, Kira in the french fry line.

"Hey, Kira."

"Hi, Diesel."

"I'm looking for Olivia. Have you seen her?"

"I thought she was with you."

"Can you text her for me? I think my phone is acting up."

Olivia texts Kira back in seconds.

"She's on the rooftop."

"Thanks."

What the hell?

Why is she avoiding me?

I find Olivia quickly, because she is the only numbskull staring into space on the rooftop in forty degree weather. I decide to sneak up on her and grab her around the waist.

"Gotcha!"

"You're an idiot."

"Tell the truth, I scared you."

"Not even a little bit."

"What are you doing up here? Thinking about jumping?" I jest.

"Thinking about life."

"What's going on? Is that nasty roommate of yours bothering you?"

"No, I dealt with her."

"Is the internship okay?"

"It's fine."

"Because you are dating one of the most popular players on the team. I think I have a little influence around here."

"I'm sure you do but that won't be necessary."

Olivia kisses me on the cheek. "You are always taking care of me."

"That's my job," I say proudly.

She slides her arms around my waist and nestles herself in my embrace. I missed this. I miss her.

"It's not your job though. I'm not that same little eleven-year-old girl that needed a friend."

"What are you talking about, JG?"

"I just want to be sure that you're happy."

"Of course I'm happy. I'd be even happier if you take me to the grill and buy me some wings. I want two orders of hot and honey barbeque. I just got out of practice. I'm starving."

"No, you're greedy."

She lifts her chin and I plant my lips firmly on her mouth. Sliding my tongue inside and claiming my kiss as if no one around us matters.

"We could skip the wings and go straight to my room if you want," I say. My voice rich with lusty need. I haven't touched Olivia in over a week which feels like a year to me.

"I have a ton of work to do."

"You can do your work at my place. I'll help you *after* we play."

"That's probably not a good idea. I'll never get anything done."

"So you don't want to come over?" I ask incredulously.

"Not tonight."

"So what was the point of me getting a single room this year if you're never in it?"

This is fucking frustrating. I feel like she is miles away when she's standing right in front of me.

"I thought you *wanted* to live by yourself."

"Yeah—to be able to freely fuck my girl."

"So your single room was about me?"

"Yes and no. Why? What's going on, JG? You're acting extra weird."

"I was thinking about the Alabama game."

"Yeah, and?"

"I think you're ready to go pro. You looked like a professional out there. You were fast, accurate, athletic. You're ready. You should enter the draft."

I look at Olivia like she has three heads. This is a

total departure from what she's been saying to me for years, and I'm not sure where it's coming from.

"Why would you want me to enter the draft?"

"It makes sense for you to capitalize on your popularity while you're hot and while you're healthy."

These aren't her words.

This isn't her.

But I'm not going to get the answers I want this way. I need her under me, and I need inside of her, and then she'll tell me everything I need to know.

"Finish your work and then come over. No matter what time. We'll talk about it then."

"Okay."

It's not until morning that I realize that I've been blown off again. I fell asleep to the Sci-Fi Channel and Olivia never showed up. She's pulling away from me, and I don't know why, but I'm not going down without a fight.

I'm about to pull out the big guns.

CHAPTER TWENTY-FOUR

I've been tired and nauseous for days.

Even though I'm on the pill now, there was a small pocket of time that Mason and I were having unprotected sex. I was so frightened that I confided in Kira.

She bought me a pregnancy test and stood right outside of the bathroom door as I peed on the stick. I've never prayed so hard in my life for God to forgive my stupidity. The last thing I need is Mason's family feeling like I've trapped him into being a father.

There was only one line.

A negative result.

My symptoms must be stress related.

My head has been spinning ever since the

conversation I had with Quincy in Alabama. It's like he laid a heavy weight of information on my chest that is bound to me. Obviously, I didn't tell Mason what he said. There would be nothing to gain from driving a wedge between him and his uncle. In fact, Mason doesn't even know that Quincy was at the game or at least that I saw him there. He never mentioned it to me, which means Quincy never said anything to him. I guess it's just as well, there's nothing I can do to change what has been done.

Mason has made decisions which have affected his entire life based on our relationship. While I am shocked and touched that he would make those considerations for me, the reality is that he is the one constantly pulling the short end of the stick. Essentially, shortchanging himself. And that is the heaviest burden for me to bear. I am the rusty anchor that is keeping this beautiful boy stuck in one place.

My stomach does a nervous somersault when I see that Mason is calling me, not because I don't want to talk to him, but because I miss him so much and I'm running out of ways to dodge him on this small campus.

"Hey, babe."

"Hey."

"You sound a little green around the gills. Are

you still not feeling well? Should I bring over some ginger ale and saltines?"

"Don't bother. I'm feeling better."

"Did you ever end up going to the campus doctor?"

"Um, yes." I lie. "I'm perfectly fine. It was probably just a bug."

"Good, because I've got a surprise for you."

Uh-oh.

"What is it?"

"It's date night."

"I didn't realize we had one of those."

"We do now and it starts tonight. Between your schedule and mine, we haven't been able to hang like we used to, so I've planned the perfect night out."

"Mason, I don't think—"

"I won't take no for an answer, JG. If you've got homework, I'll help you with it later. Be ready by six."

"Don't you do the midnight run with the team tonight?"

"I think I've earned a night off don't you?"

"But you really like the midnight run."

"I like a lot of things, but I like you more."

"You're too much."

"You should know that better than anyone."

The problem is, I do.

"Six o'clock, babe, and dress sexy for me."

He's relentless. There will be no talking him out of this date night. I'm going to have to pull myself together and go.

"I'll be ready."

I'M NOT REALLY SURE HOW A PLAIN JERSEY GIRL like me got so lucky. I've snagged myself a boyfriend who is gorgeous, funny, smart, is going to take our team to the championship *and* finds the time to plan dates for us.

Mason arrives at my dorm dressed in a pair of new jeans, a soft brown turtleneck, and dark tan boots. I can't help but be excited to see him, especially when he looks like this, so I hug him harder than usual.

"Now this is the reaction I was looking for," he says while nuzzling the crook of my neck.

"You smell good," I tell him.

"You should like how I smell. You bought me the body wash three years in a row for Christmas."

He moves me away from him to take a look at my outfit.

"And you wore my favorite jeans. Your ass looks amazing in those, babe. Thank you."

I chuckle.

"You have a one track mind."

"You're right. It's always on you. Now let's go," he says after checking the time on his phone. "We're sticking to a strict schedule tonight."

We sit in the back of a cab on our way to who knows where. Mason wants to keep everything a secret like he's carrying out some sort of clandestine mission. I don't mind, it's kind of fun. We soon arrive in front of a place called The Light Factory. I've heard of it before but have never been inside. It's a downtown event space that apparently has a line of people shivering outside of it.

"We're here!"

Mason grabs my hand excitedly as we walk by the line and to the front where the Will Call desk is.

"Two tickets for Bridgewater."

"ID please."

It's obvious that we're here for a concert, but I can't tell who we're seeing. This space is unique. There are no posters hanging up, no flyers scattered around, just lights. Lot and lots of lights.

"You want anything to eat, JG?"

"I want to know who we're seeing."

"Okay." He chuckles. "Let's find our seats then."

As soon as we step inside it all makes sense. I see two women sitting in vintage Thunder Road T-shirts and I scream.

"You didn't!"

"I did," he says proudly.

"How did you get the tickets? You're a broke college student."

"I called in a favor."

I look at our tickets to find our actual seats. They're really good ones. I'm going to see Tommy, John, Ward, Bobby, and Max up front and in living color. If I was the girly type, I'd be crying right now.

"I'm surprised you didn't know they were in town, Jersey girl. You have to be the biggest fan these weirdos have."

"I guess it got past me."

Mason gives me a look of concern.

"Don't let the pressure of school distract you from everything else that matters, babe."

It's obvious he's talking about us.

"I won't."

"Promise me."

"I promise."

He pulls me into his embrace.

"Now what do you have to say to me?"

"Thank you?"

"That's it?"

"You're the best boyfriend a girl could have?"

"That's without saying."

"I love you?"

"You're almost there."

I laugh to myself.

"Refreshments are on me."

He smiles wide and plants a huge kiss on my lips.

"That's more like it. Let's go get my hot dogs, popcorn, and two beers. I'm going to need 'em to get through ninety minutes of these guys."

I kiss Mason again and almost skip my way to the refreshment stand.

CHAPTER TWENTY-FIVE

Senior year

Christmas in Bear Springs is a beloved holiday. The streets of the shopping areas are lined with maple trees covered in white lights and Christmas carols are playing through strategically placed outdoor speakers. Store counters are covered with tinsel and Christmas tchotchkes, and people are especially friendly.

Normally during Christmas break, I don't get to spend much of it with Olivia or my family because I'm getting ready for some sort of football game. This year coach decided that since we're on a championship run that we will pass on playing in Georgia's Peach Blossom Bowl and stay focused on our mission. That means that all of my days are busy with practice, but my nights are my own.

"You want to go to The Red Lion tonight?"

My buddies Simon, Pete, and I have talked about hanging somewhere local and maybe seeing some of our friends from high school. It might be a little arrogant to say, but we're kind of like celebrities to some of them. Hometown boys who may be National Champions in a matter of weeks.

"Yeah, let's go."

"Is Olivia coming?"

"I don't think so. She wanted to spend some time with her mom tonight. Help out decorating the house."

"I can't believe you two are still together after all this time."

"That's my girl."

"What are y'all going to do when the draft comes?" Pete asks.

"What do you mean?"

"Is she going to follow you wherever you end up?"

Olivia and I haven't talked about the draft. It's been a sore subject for us since freshman year. She's always said it's because of my safety that she didn't want me to go early, but I think it's always been about the fact that we'd be apart. She's just too up her own ass to realize it. She'd miss me. Plain and simple.

"I don't think that far ahead, man, but we'll be together whatever happens."

"Good thing you dodged that bullet last year," Simon says.

"What bullet?"

"The pregnancy thing."

My pulse accelerates at an alarming rate.

"What pregnancy thing, Simon?"

Pete averts his eyes from mine. Simon's enlarge. "Maybe I—"

"Don't backpedal now. Spill it, you fuckwad."

"Damn, D, I don't know if I should be the one telling you this."

"But you are."

"You know I was fucking Kira last year for a while."

"Yeah."

"She bought Jersey girl a pregnancy test last year. I didn't ask her any more about it because she was so upset that she told me at all. She felt like she betrayed her friend. I assumed that if she was actually pregnant that she, you know, took care of it because I didn't hear any more about it."

I'm going to be sick.

This explains why she was nauseous for weeks. Why she was avoiding me. Why she wasn't fucking me. Why everything was magically better after seeing the doctor.

I feel like I can't breathe. How could she do this?

"I don't know who she is anymore," I say, not meaning to say it out loud, but I can't help it. She has wrecked me.

"She didn't tell you?"

"Not a fucking word."

"Maybe you should talk to her, D," Pete says.

"The time for talking was last year."

"I know but—"

"I want to get drunk."

They both shake their heads in disapproval.

"Not a good idea, D."

"Okay then, if you bozos won't do it, then I'll drive."

I'M ALMOST GOOD AND DRUNK AFTER THREE beers and four shots of tequila when Olivia texts me.

Olivia: Are you having fun?

Me: Yep

Olivia: Are you okay?

Me: Yep

Olivia: Are a lot of people there from school?

Me: Yep

Olivia: What's up with these one word answers. Am I freakin' bothering you?!

Me: Yep

I order another round of shots when Ginger saunters her way over to me. She looks good in an over-the-top kind of way that she always did. Lots of makeup, lots of hair, and lots of cleavage. She could never hold a candle to Olivia's natural beauty, which is why I never sealed the deal with her.

"Hi there, superstar."

"Hi to you too."

"You're looking fantastic as usual."

"You too. You want a drink?"

Her smile brightens.

"Sure, I'll take a seven and seven."

"What the hell is that?"

"It's my mom's drink, and I ended up liking it."

"Seven and seven for the lady, please." She hops up on the stool beside me. "So where are you now?"

"I'm at Duke."

"Nice."

"I'm in a five-year program though, so I won't be graduating this year."

"What are you studying?"

"Physical therapy."

"Sweet."

"Who knows," she speaks seductively while rubbing her hands along one of my biceps. "Maybe I'll work with athletes."

"Maybe you will, Ginger snap."

I throw back another shot.

"What are you doing after this?" Ginger has never been shy and gets straight to the point. "You want to finally know firsthand why they call me that?"

Oh shit, I giggle to myself, did she know about her nickname?

"I, um—"

I'm tempted but the next thing that pops into my head is Olivia's face. As angry as I am, as hurt as I am, as heartbroken as I am if she did kill our baby; I know that I love her. No matter what her level of betrayal is, I refuse to stoop lower.

"I'm just going to hang back here with my boys."

"Aw, but you're with Simon and Pete all of the time."

"You're welcome to hang out with me at the bar, Ginger, but I'm not leaving."

"That's fine. I'll just hang."

Ginger and I end up reminiscing about some of the times we hung out in school and teachers that we both had. With every additional drink she gets more handsy, and I grow more tolerant of it, but I never cross the line.

A popular slow song from high school comes on and a few couples take to the Lion's small dance floor.

"You wanna dance?" she asks.

"I'm too drunk."

"You owe me a dance. You dumped me at the Harvest Festival, remember?"

"I did do that, didn't I."

"You sure did. I was mortified."

"Guess I owe you a dance then."

When I stand up it's like every drink I had tonight rushes to my head. I'm seeing doubles of everyone, but I'm still clear-headed enough to sway to a corny ballad. Ginger curls her arms around my waist, and I wrap mine around her neck, almost leaning a bit of my drunken weight onto her because I'm going to have to if I'm going to last this whole song.

"Don't worry, I've got you," she says.

We sway for a minute and I close my eyes as our movement and the slow tempo of the song lull me practically to sleep. When it's over, my eyes pop back open and the floor almost drops from below my feet.

Olivia is staring straight at me with a look that could kill.

"You fucker."

"Olivia–."

She runs straight for the door and I push Ginger to the side and try running after her, but I'm too sloshed. I see like three doors, and I pick the wrong one. Running straight into the wall and down to the floor like the loser that I am.

OLIVIA

"Olivia, would you turn that crap off!"

I have been playing the same Thunder Road song through my new Bluetooth speaker for the last hour. It's a ballad that Max sang about hating the girl who broke his heart for the first time. I can relate. For the first time in my life, I cried over Mason Bridgewater last night.

"I'm using my Christmas gift," I yell back downstairs to her. My mom gifted me a Bluetooth speaker for Christmas that has amazing sound.

"I can hear that, but could you change the song?"

"No."

In fifteen minutes, my mom has seemed to have had enough and knocks on my door. I open it with an attitude and a tear-stained face. Where are my rights? If I want to listen to Thunder Road for the next three days, I should be able to.

"What—"

But it's not my mother—it's Mason.

He looks tired, and hungover, and sad.

"Can we talk?"

"There's nothing to talk about," I say.

He doesn't listen and pushes his way in, closing the door behind him.

"My mother doesn't like closed doors with boys in the room."

"She's made an exception today, because you were killing her with Thunder Road on repeat."

"Say what you've come to say."

"What you saw last night ... it wasn't what it looked like."

"Really? Because it looked like you had your mitts all over Ginger."

"I was drunk, and it looked worse than it was. I promise you."

"I came out last night, because I knew something wasn't right. Your texts were abrupt and rude and I had to see for myself why. You were too busy sniffing behind her skanky ass."

"Were you pregnant last year?"

"What?"

"I asked you if were you pregnant last year?"

"No."

"Tell me the truth, Olivia!"

"I am telling you the truth."

"Did you think you were pregnant?"

"Yes."

"But you weren't?"

"No."

"And you're being honest with me."

"You think I'm lying? You think I *what* ... had an abortion?"

"I don't know. You've been acting strange for months. I just don't know."

"Wow."

"Well, if you thought you were pregnant then why didn't you tell me?"

"I didn't want you to worry, and I was right not to tell you, because it was a false alarm."

"No, you were not fucking right. You should have told me, so we could have worried together. If you had been pregnant it would have been *our* responsibility, not just yours."

"Let's just suppose for a second that I had been pregnant. What would we have done?"

"We would have raised our baby together."

"With what money?"

"With the money I would have received once I'd been drafted."

"So you would have entered the draft early?"

"Yes!"

I rub my face with my hands with frustration.

"That wasn't your plan."

"Plans change."

"Seems like your plans always change when it comes to me."

"What the fuck does that mean?"

"Did you even want to go to Union, Mason?"

"Of course."

"Was it your first choice?"

He pauses before he answers. Searching my face for the meaning behind my question.

"Yes."

"You're lying."

"Fine, no, it wasn't my first choice."

"Why did you choose to go?"

"It was free."

"Was there any other reason?"

"Because you were going there."

"I didn't know that you got into Stanford. I didn't know that you had a free ride to Stanford to play ball."

"I wasn't going all the way to California, Olivia. Stanford was never a consideration."

"It would have been the best option."

"I took us to the championships last year, and I'm taking us this year. I think this was a great option. There are five pro teams interested in me. Our future is set."

"What if I don't get a job where you end up signing?"

"You'll find one. There are publicity jobs everywhere. I could probably get you one with whatever team I sign with once I'm in there."

"What if that's not what I want to do?"

"What?"

"My life cannot constantly revolve around yours. I have to make my own way and so do you. I don't want you making any more decisions based on what's going on with me. I feel like a burden, Mason. Like an anchor weighing you down. I know you're going to say I'm crazy, but that's how I feel. You help me with everything, and I give you nothing."

Mason wraps his hand around my neck and pulls me into him.

"Are you fucking kidding me? You give me everything. You are my greatest cheerleader, my best friend, my confidant. You are not an anchor, you are my lifesaver."

"I'm sorry," I try turning away from him. "But I've made my decision."

"What decision?"

"I wish you the best wherever you end up, but I'm not going to follow you."

Mason takes a deep breath to keep from yelling. I can tell he is fed up with this conversation and doesn't like at all where it's headed.

"So you want to try the long distance thing for a while?"

"That's not what I'm saying."

"Then I need you to be crystal fucking clear. What are you saying?"

"I'm saying that my head is all messed up. That maybe we should take a break."

"A break."

"Yes."

"Is this about last night? I told you I didn't touch Ginger. We danced, but that was it, and I'm sorry that I even did that, but you know me. You know there is no one in this world for me but you. It's always been you. It will always be you."

My heart is breaking.

This is not at all what I want, but it's what we

both need, and for once I have to be the strong one. For once, I need to make the sacrifice.

"I want to break up."

He looks like he's struggling between the thought of strangling me or kissing me.

"None of this shit means anything if you don't want to be around to share it with me."

"I hope that's not true, because you are weeks away from winning the national championship."

"You're my best friend," he states in an almost desperate plea.

I have to remember why I'm doing this. I have to be strong.

"I still think we need to break up."

"So this is your final decision?"

"Yes."

"Then you are making a big fucking mistake."

He slams the door when he leaves my room, abruptly apologizes to my mother, and then jumps in his SUV and skids away.

"What happened?" My mother asks as she dabs the tears streaming down my face with a tissue.

"I think I finally freed the anchor."

FOURTH QUARTER

CHAPTER TWENTY-SEVEN

"Are you finished with your bagel?"

My supervisor, Paula, peeps her head into my cubicle workspace. Her reading glasses perched on her head, pushing her curly gray bob away from her face, and there's a look of anxiety spread across her forehead.

"Totally."

I push away the last few bites of my bagel. I'm not really finished with my lightly toasted, everything bagel, but it's not like I could tell her to come back in fifteen minutes. She's my boss.

"Then can I see you in my office?"

"Of course, I'll be right in."

I grab my steaming hot, jumbo mug of English

Breakfast tea like it's a life preserver and head into Paula's office.

"Have a seat," she says while simultaneously clearing her throat. It seems to be one of her small tics that appears when she's uncomfortable. "I wanted to talk to you briefly about something before we head into the meeting."

Paula shuts her door before she sits back down, which is highly unusual. I've only worked here a few brief months, but I already know that she keeps her office door open so that she can eavesdrop on everyone's phone calls.

She isn't a mean boss or anything, but she's old school, and doesn't believe in people taking personal calls during work hours. It's the quickest way to get on her bad side, although I haven't quite figured out why that is, considering that she has four kids and a husband herself. She has the fullest personal life out of everyone in this office. She should know and understand that sometimes stuff happens and you have to make a personal call.

I take a seat across from her desk, cross my legs, and take a delicate sip of my tea to feign confidence. The truth is that I'm shaking in my boots. This job means everything to me, and not just because of a paycheck, but because I love what I do.

"What's going on?" I ask, cutting right to the chase.

"As you know two of our high-profile players are on suspension for substance abuse."

"Collins and Matthews."

"This is the second time for Collins. It's a shame really, but anyway, the front office is going to be looking for a big plan from us to clean up the club's image."

"I think we should be able to come up with something. Community service blitz maybe?"

"We'll hammer out the details later, but I'm giving you a heads up for another reason. I think the owner wants us to focus our energies on the new guy—Bridgewater. You went to college with him, right?"

It's only been two weeks since I discovered that he's been traded to the Nighthawks, but I knew his name was bound to come up sooner or later. Today is the day, and I feel even worse than I thought I would to hear his name.

"I did, yes."

"I've tried reaching out to him already, but he hasn't responded. Some players are skittish about doing PR tours, but I thought since he's looking for a fresh start that he'd be more than willing to do a few

PR events for us. It would be great if he did. He's so easy on the eyes isn't he?"

"Yep."

I take another sip of my tea to make sure that I can actually still swallow. My throat is tightening up just thinking about the possibility of working with Mason, but I've endured five separate interviews to get this job and I'm not going to risk losing it just because of an old flame.

Paula begins speaking in a much lower voice as if she's telling me a very guarded secret.

"Now, you know I had the final say on getting you hired, Olivia. That's why I pulled you in here today to tell you ahead of the meeting. If you've got any tricks up your sleeve, any rabbits you can pull out of a hat, then now is the time. This ball club seems to only be in the news when bad things happen, and that looks poorly on our department's performance. You understand what I'm saying?"

I hear her loud and clear. Paula's worked her ass off to become the head of our publicity department. A first for a woman in the league. We have to work harder and be better than the other PR departments that are run by men, or the powers that be will seek to replace us and they won't think twice about it.

"I totally understand."

What Paula doesn't know is that I was in love with this man for most of my life and that he probably hates me. Why do I think that? Because I've reached out to him a couple of times but haven't heard one word back from him in five years, and my mother still lives next door to his parents in Bear Springs.

I'm not sure how it's possible that we've stayed off of each other's radars, and out of each other's way, but we have. Regardless—I'm going to have to figure out a way to work with him, because like it or not, I need this to succeed.

"All right then, let's get to it."

I take a huge gulp of my tea as if it contains some sort of miraculous power source and follow behind my mentor into the biggest meeting of my life.

CHAPTER TWENTY-EIGHT

Paula ends up presenting the entire room with a thorough overview of a six-month publicity plan that should offset the bad coverage we've been getting lately. It's a solid plan involving public television spots, traditional sports news interviews, and a pitch to HBO to be the focus of their next reality sports documentary television series, *Hard Knocks*. But I can tell by the stoic faces in the room that they aren't impressed.

"It's a long tail plan, and I think that everyone here was hoping for a more immediate solution."

"We just don't have another six months for all of this to hopefully kick in."

Jim Tessa reports directly to the NHL and never lets us forget it. While the teams are individually owned, much like a franchise, there are certain standards and rules that each team has to abide by. Code of conduct is one.

"I hear you, but where was all this urgency when you were screening for illegal substances?" Paula counters. She's a tough cookie and will not be walked all over. I love that about her.

"It's your job to put out fires."

"That would be much easier to do if we had one squeaky clean player we could rely on to offset the bad coverage."

"I don't know if any of that matters. You are the spin doctor. You should be able to make us look like saints even if we have a team full of sinners."

"So what do you propose, Jim?" Paula's tone strains to remain respectful. "I'm dying to know."

I take another sip of tea watching the lively exchange as if it's a tennis match. Then Jim suddenly turns his eyes toward me.

"The answer is so clear, that I'm amazed no one else has brought it up yet."

"Please share," Paula says.

"You're an alumnus of Georgia Union, right Olivia?" he asks me.

"Um, yes."

Paula looks at me and winks. I take another sip of

my tea. She knew that they were going to ask me about this. She may have even planned it. I don't know her well enough to be sure, but I do know that she is a master manipulator. Anything is possible.

"May I ask why no one has thought of the obvious?"

Paula sighs heavily with frustration. "Which is?"

"Putting Diesel Bridgewater out front. I mean like seriously plastering his panty dropping smile all over New York. Let's get him on television, sides of buses, subway stations, soup kitchens, children's hospitals. Everywhere."

The tea in my belly begins to churn forcefully inside of me like a tsunami when I think of it all.

"It can be your new hire's first big campaign. I know Union is a small school. She must have known him if she worked as a team publicist. We paid a lot of money to buy his contract, and he owes us, but you know how temperamental these players are. He'll probably be more likely to follow her lead since they have a shared history."

"Not sure if it's going to happen, Jim. I've reached out to him numerous times, but the guy hasn't responded to any of our communications."

"Maybe that's because the communication hasn't come from Olivia," Jim responds.

Crap.

I've worked really hard to make sure that no one at any university I've worked for or the NFL knew about my connection to Mason. Basically, for this very reason. I assumed that if they knew, that they'd eventually want me to call in a favor. Something I would never do. Something that at this rate is almost impossible for me to do. He won't talk to me, and I don't blame him.

"What do you mean?" Paula stares curiously at me. "So what, they went to Union together? I went to Michigan, but you don't see me exchanging Christmas cards with Tom Brady."

"I knew Mason in college," I interject. Trying to salvage any little bit of credibility I have left with Paula. "I knew him well."

A few people around the table start muttering under their breath.

"That's what I heard," Jim says with a grin on his face like a cat who swallowed a canary. "In fact, I heard you two grew up together in Georgia. Next-door neighbors right?"

This is disastrous for me. I should have told Paula about this when she brought me into her office. Now we've both been blindsided in front of our bosses.

"I'm sure our relationship has been exaggerated by whoever told you about it," I say. "I haven't spoken to him in a very long time. Plus, I'm not even sure that getting him involved would be helpful."

"What do you mean it wouldn't be helpful?" Jim challenges. "Diesel is photographed everywhere he goes. He has at least two endorsement commercials being aired as we speak. One is for the Under Armor clothing line, and the other is for a sports drink, plus he *always* has a hot actress or singer on his arm. He could bring tremendous visibility to the ball club if we could use his celebrity as leverage."

"You probably have your reasons for keeping the fact that you have a connection to Mason Bridgewater to yourself, Olivia, but if there is any chance you could ask him to get on board—I can't see how it wouldn't *matter*," Paula adds with a bit of salt in her voice.

She's definitely pissed at me.

"I might be able to convince him to cooperate," I say. Immediately wishing that I could swallow my desperate words completely back down my throat the minute they fall out of my mouth. Especially because Paula's eyes light up with hope.

I've done it now.

"That's awesome," Jim says as he adjusts his

rather large frame in the conference table chair. Making the base of the seat squeak when he does. "I'll put him in touch with you. He's definitely got some down time on his hands, since he's still recovering from his injury."

I can feel Paula's proud stare from across the table, and it makes me feel a little uneasy. It's going to be such a long shot if I can actually get Mason to agree to anything, but like Paula alluded to earlier, I'm in here fighting for my job today. Maybe for the entire department's jobs.

"I just want to be clear about what I'm asking him to do."

"Anything," Paula cuts in with a wide grin across her mouth. I mean she's showing teeth and everything. "Whatever you can get him to agree to. I'll put together a kick ass, short-term plan of attack."

The general manager, Mr. Kirkpatrick, has been silent the entire meeting but now hits the table with his palm.

"This will work," he states matter-of-factly with a pleased gleam in his eyes. "Meeting adjourned."

After the conference room empties, Paula pats me on the shoulder to stop me from leaving.

"Why didn't you mention that you knew Bridgewater?"

"It's complicated."

"Did you sleep with him in college?"

I don't want to tell her that it's even worse than that.

"Yes."

"Hell, that could work to your advantage. I've never MET a man that didn't want to come back for a second taste."

"I'm not sure he'd be interested."

"Did you give him the clap?"

"No." I giggle.

"You're beautiful, he's single, and if I wasn't so long in the tooth—I'd do the dirty job myself." She laughs.

But I don't laugh.

All of a sudden, nothing is funny anymore.

All of a sudden, I just want to vomit.

"Damn, Bridgewater, you look like my Grandpappy out there!"

"You're never going to catch a ball running that slow."

"Diesel my ballsack. We should nickname you sludge."

My new teammates seem to enjoy busting my balls. I know what a lot of them are thinking. I was hailed as the second coming in the NFL but when I got here, I didn't do much. My stats are abysmal, my body hurts every day, and I can't get a quarterback in this league to throw me the ball.

On the other hand, thanks to Uncle Quincy, I make a lot of money. I have really great endorsement deals, have done two animation voiceover parts, and taped five scenes on a new television medical drama.

"Stop lying to yourself," I say out of breath. "I can outrun your fat asses any day."

"Outrun us to McDonald's."

"Bridgewater." The coach calls me off of the field with a look of disgust on his face. "Hit the showers. You have a meeting with pub department."

"I do?"

"Something Kirkpatrick hooked up. You gotta at least take the meeting."

"Coach, I'm trying to focus all my energies on getting back in shape."

"I totally agree but what do you want me to do? There are parts of this job that ain't fun. Meet with 'em. You don't have to do anything you don't want to, but you have to give them the courtesy of doing their job."

"All right, coach."

I jog off the field, take a quick shower, and go to the player's club area of the stadium. At least I'll be able to grab a seafood platter while I listen to whatever crap that I won't be doing.

"Hey, Diesel."

"Hi, Martha. I think I'm meeting the pub people

here today. Can I get a seafood platter and two glasses of apple juice in the booth over there?"

"I'll put the order in now. I think I saw the woman you're meeting with head to the restroom. She'll be right back. She ordered a grilled chicken sandwich."

I'm answering emails when I hear the loud clicking of heels against the stone-tiled floor coming toward me. When I turn and see who it is, it's like all the oxygen in the room has been sucked completely out and I'm spinning into a time vortex.

It's Olivia.

That cold-hearted bitch.

She is stunning.

Her breasts seem fuller, her ass sits round and high, and her hair falls in long luscious coils past her shoulders. She's wearing a fitted V-neck sweater, some black leggings underneath, and a pair of thigh-high, high-heeled boots that make my dick hard.

"Hello, Mason."

I don't respond.

I just gawk.

I want to rip off all of her clothes and fuck her senseless in the middle of this lounge.

She slides into the other side of the booth.

"I know what you're thinking," she says in a guarded tone.

"I seriously doubt that."

"I got this job before you were traded here. I even thought about quitting once I heard you were coming but—"

"You love football too much to ever give up this job."

"You're right ... I do."

"So what is this meeting about?"

"The club wants a targeted PR campaign with you in the center of it."

"Do you have a manager position already?"

"No."

"So this is personal."

She shuts her eyes tightly and exhales.

"They found out that we were neighbors. They're using me in hopes that you'll cooperate. Most players don't want to do the PR tours. It can take up a lot of your off time."

"Do they know anything else about us?" I ask in my best icy voice.

"No."

Martha walks over with the food.

"Grilled chicken for the lady and seafood platter for the wide receiver."

I wink at Martha.

"Thanks, babe."

"I see you're still a favorite with the ladies," she uncomfortably jokes.

"I see you still like a grilled chicken sandwich."

"You don't?"

"No, my tastes have elevated."

I mean that as a jab, but I'm sorry I said it as soon as the words fly out of my mouth. I don't want to hurt her, but I don't want to make this easy either. This woman broke my fucking heart, and I'll never let her back in.

She pulls a notebook out of her bag.

"There are a few events we thought you would be a great fit for. I can go over them if you like. See if you're interested in participating."

"What's in it for me?" I say as I pop a grilled shrimp in my mouth.

I laugh as a thin layer of sweat forms on the tip of her nose. She was always hot and always messy.

"The way I see it, you need this publicity just as badly as the team does."

"Is that right?"

"You've struggled a bit since you've entered the league."

"Have I?"

"It's not totally your fault."

"It's not my fault at all. I've been injured."

"Well, yes, and no. You also don't get along with any of your quarterbacks."

"Because those asshats don't throw me the ball when I'm wide open."

"You have to have chemistry."

"It's a simple game. You throw the ball to the open man on the field. We don't need to be best friends for that. And guess what? You're not my football guru anymore. I don't need your advice or guidance. I need you to tell me what you're here for and then go about your business like you have for the last five fucking years."

There's an uncomfortable silence between us. Then she speaks.

"I tried calling you. The day you were drafted. Then the day you went to Arizona. Then the day your dad had the heart attack."

"Must have been my service acting janky," I lie.

"I figured it was something like that."

"So ... continue."

She takes a bite of her sandwich.

"It would be a series of publicity shoots, late night talk show appearances, and some autograph signings at local community events."

"How long would this take?"

"There would be a six-month commitment, and if your schedule allowed it then maybe longer."

A blob of ketchup spills on her sweater and she doesn't even see it. I lean over with a napkin and wipe it off.

"Still messy as usual."

Her body tenses, and she doesn't respond.

My hand lingers a little longer than it should.

"Are you going to be at all these events?" I ask her.

"I'm afraid so."

My dick applauds.

"I'll commit to three events to start with and then we'll see after that."

"That's fair."

A pretty smile spreads on her face. It's a smile that I've missed with every fiber in my body. I used to do whatever I could to see that smile. Especially when we were making love. It's addictive.

"There you are!"

Like a glass of cold water, Sarah walks into the lounge and wakes me the hell up. Her greeting reminds me of where I am and who I am. There is no Diesel and Jersey girl anymore. We are not in college shooting the shit at The End Zone. We are two grown people who have moved on in the real world.

"Hey," I greet Sarah with a kiss on the cheek.

"The trainers said you were in here. Who's this?"

She takes a seat next to me.

"This is Olivia. She works Nighthawk publicity. Olivia, this is my girl Sarah."

Olivia looks completely shocked. Maybe it's because she didn't think I'd be seeing anyone, or maybe it's because she knows Sarah from somewhere but she isn't sure where. That's because Sarah is a known character actress. She's one of those actresses that you've seen a million times in shows, but you don't ever quite catch their real names.

"Nice to meet you."

Sarah extends her hand to Olivia. They shake hands, but it doesn't get past me that Olivia wipes it on her leggings.

"Likewise."

"Is this the Olivia that you grew up with, Diesel?"

"Yes, that's me."

"I've heard a lot about you. You played football with D, and Simon, and Pete when you were kids, right? You were like their little mascot. Their little warrior."

"That's a way to put it." Olivia stands up.

"Well, Mason, I'll be in contact with you to schedule the first event. It will probably be something for PBS. It was good seeing you and nice meeting you, Sarah."

"You should come to the housewarming!" Sarah blurts out.

I could stop this before it goes too far, but I'd rather just let it play out.

"Housewarming?"

"Had to move to the big city now that D is playing here. It's a great place with amazing views."

"Oh, so did I. I bet yours is nicer though."

"It's definitely nice. We'd love to have you. I'm sure the guys will be excited to see you too."

"Well, um—"

"I don't think Olivia has time for that, love. She's probably really busy with her new job. It's pretty much all she cares about."

Olivia glares at me with those two mismatched eyes of hers.

"Nope," she says through gritted teeth. "I think I can make it. Send me the details."

CHAPTER THIRTY

"What a clusterfuck."

"I realize that, Kira."

"Put the phone closer to your mouth. I can't hear enough of your stinky attitude."

"Hardy, har, har."

"You're not actually going to that housewarming thing are you?"

"I am."

"Just a few weeks ago you told me you were over him."

"And I am over him."

"Then why are you going over to his apartment that he shares with his *girlfriend?* What are you trying to do? Punish yourself for breaking up with him?"

"He was just in the news with some other chick. How could that teeny tiny actress be his real girlfriend? She's not his type at all."

"And your point? Why are you so concerned about what his type is if you're over him?"

"I'm not. Forget I mentioned her. I just want to show him that we will be able to work together just fine, and that I'm a grown-ass woman, and that I've moved on."

"You are setting yourself up, *chica*. This isn't going to end well for you."

"It will be fine. I'll have one drink, a few hors d'oeuvres, because I know there will be a ton of them, and then I'll leave."

"Keep it classy."

I always do.

MASON AND SARAH LIVE IN A BEAUTIFULLY decorated penthouse apartment on the Upper West Side. I'm surprised though, because it's a very sleek, modern apartment with a lot of his memorabilia displayed around the main living areas—not a lot of traditional feminine touches, and she looks like the type that would have floral shit everywhere.

I'm wearing a soft pink, sleeveless dress that is fitted in the bodice and flares below the waist. It has lots of movement and best of all it pops against the color of my skin. I wanted to look pretty, but I also wanted to make sure that I didn't look like I was trying too hard. I think I succeeded.

"Jersey girl!"

Simon and Pete yell my old nickname from across the room. As soon as I see them, I remember just how much I miss those fatheads. They were a pain in the butt when we were younger, but they grew to be really nice guys. I was sad when I lost them in the breakup, but they always belonged to Mason. They were his friends first.

"Hi, guys."

"Shit, look at you. You're wearing dresses now?"

"I'm a lady." I laugh. "So you better act right."

"Then let me get the lady a drink. Mason's pulled out all the good liquor tonight."

"Then I'll take a little Prosecco."

"Coming right up."

As Pete goes over to the bar, I catch up with Simon.

"So I hear you work for the Nighthawks now."

"Yeah, I got the job with the publicity department a couple of months ago."

"And you'll be working with our boy?"

"Just a little."

"He's had a tough go of things so far in the league."

"I've read some stuff. I'm aware."

"What you read is only half of the story. When you left him, you broke his heart, Olivia. He became someone unrecognizable. He's always injured now because he doesn't take good care of himself. It's not like back when you were in his life to make sure that he did. There's no accountability."

"Is that how you saw it? That I took care of him?"

"Of course—Mason was totally dependent on your crazy ass. His uncle and his dad had good intentions, but sometimes they pressured him too much. They always saw big lights and dollar signs when they talked football with him. You saw the love of the game. And you simply saw Mason."

I look at Simon and say with a crack in my voice, "I loved him, Simon."

"I know you did."

"I hope he's happy with her."

"What do you mean?"

"This housewarming. Their relationship. It's a

big step for him to move in with somebody. He must be happy."

Simon laughs at me.

"You think they live together?"

"Of course."

"This is a housewarming for D. The two of them are just fuck buddies."

"But she said *our* new digs, and he didn't correct her."

"You might want to think about why he did that."

"Because he hates me."

"Maybe he should, but that's not the truth. He loves you, Olivia. He's never stopped loving you."

I take another stroll around the living room, the dining room, and the den of the apartment. A careful look this time. There are photos of Mason at the creek where we used to play, the old football field in the village, the Snake's Tongue bike trail, one of his highest receiving yard high school games, and a framed menu from The End Zone at Georgia Union. I may be missing from all of the photos, but I was there. I was at every single place and share more than one memory of the both of us at all of the locations.

I want to check one more thing, but the door to his bedroom is closed. I want to be certain that this is not this woman's house. I know what Simon said, and he has no reason to lie to me, but I need to be sure.

I open what I assume is the door to the master bedroom, but it's not. It's a small office area. I blink several times when I notice what's hanging on the wall above a small wooden desk made of oak.

It's a Thunder Road platinum album.

Mounted and displayed in what appears to be a very expensive and gigantic frame.

"I bought that with my first big check."

Mason's deep voice rumbles behind me and my stomach flips like I am seventeen again.

"How much was it?"

"A lot of fucking money. I got it from a Christie's auction."

"Why did you buy it?"

"I don't know. Showing off I guess."

"It's beautiful."

"Do you want it?"

"I couldn't take a gift like that."

Mason walks closer behind me.

"I wanted to give you stuff like that and more. I wanted to give you everything." I can feel his hard body on my ass. His breath on my neck. "But you destroyed it."

He closes the door behind him.

"Mason."

"Turn around, Olivia."

I slowly turn around to face him, but I can't meet his eyes. I'm too ashamed. Too full of regrets. I handled things badly five years ago.

"Look at me," he demands. "Why are you here tonight?"

"To congratulate you and Sarah."

"Liar." He sneers.

"To show you we can work together."

"Liar."

I start biting my lip. There are words swirling around in my head. Words that I wish I was brave enough to say. I just can't get them out.

"Be the girl I met when I was eleven years old. The girl so tough that she played tackle football with a bunch of boys she'd never met before. Be brave. Say what it is you've come to say."

Tears begin to cloud my eyes.

The words are still stuck inside of me.

Mason pulls me into him and places a kiss on each of my eyelids.

"These are the most beautiful eyes I've ever seen. This one"—he kisses my left lid—"is larger than the other." Then he kisses the right.

I wrap my arms around his waist and hug him so tightly that he may not be able to ever breathe again.

"I missed you so much, Mason," I say. "I'm sorry for what I did to us."

He plunks his head on top of mine and exhales a heavy breath.

"Finally."

I try to stop myself, but the tears just start to fall, and I'm crying hysterically now. Sobbing like a little girl as I lean dead in the center of my best friend's chest.

There is quiet between us as he uses a finger to play with my hair while he waits patiently for me to release all of the regret and guilt that I've had pent up.

"I shouldn't of broken up with you," I say resolutely.

"You're right. You shouldn't have."

"I was young and dumb and not as confident as I pretended to be. I thought I was doing the right thing."

"Leaving me was the opposite of the right thing."

"You were making decisions that were not best for you."

"You're right, I was making decisions that were best for *us*."

"Junior year–"

"Junior year we had a pregnancy scare. Kids in college who are fucking like bunny rabbits have pregnancy scares, Olivia."

"No, that's not what I'm talking about."

He stops winding my hair around his finger and lifts my chin up to meet his gaze.

"I'm sorry. I shouldn't have interrupted. Tell me. What are you talking about?"

"I talked to your uncle."

"When? About what?"

"He came to the Arizona game junior year. He brought an NFL scout there, which I knew you didn't know about. I confronted him about it, but then he proceeded to tell me everything you'd done because of me. Everything you gave up because of me. Not taking scholarships with Stanford and Michigan. Not entering the draft–"

"What could have possibly made you think that I wasn't doing what I wanted to do? That I wasn't right where I wanted to be? This football thing was our dream, not just mine."

"But he was so convincing."

"You should have known better. My uncle doesn't speak for me. He never has. He's just a man trying to inflate his own sense of self importance by living vicariously through me. He should have never spoken to you like that, and trust me when I say that he will never do that shit again."

"It was a long time ago, Mason."

"You're damn straight it was. Too long. Years that we could have been together. Time that we've wasted. I've been miserable without you, JG."

"Not as miserable as I've been. I missed you so much, Mason."

As my crying slows down, Mason sits me down on the bed, and walks across the room and locks the door.

"What are you doing, Mason?" I whisper.

He says nothing as he bends down and starts taking off my shoes one at a time. He lightly massages each foot and starts using his hands to slowly knead my legs.

I am breathless by the time he slides his hands under my dress and reaches the crease of my thighs and hips. He looks up at me with surprise once he realizes that I'm not wearing any underwear, and it flips a switch on inside of him that I vividly remember from years ago.

He wants me.

With almost brute force he slides my hips forward on the bed and maneuvers his head underneath my dress. Growling as he kisses the inside of my thighs and rubs the lips of my sex with his fingers.

"I have been dreaming about this pussy for five fucking years." He snarls fiercely into my skin. "This fat, wet, pussy."

I immediately become drenched in between my legs.

"It seems like it's been dreaming about me too," he says in a voice thick with need. "Look how happy she is to see me."

He devours me like he is eating his favorite meal. Like it's delicious and desires seconds and maybe thirds. It doesn't take long before my legs begin to shake as I try to hold my orgasm at bay.

"Not yet," he barks at me. "Not fucking yet."

He comes out from under my dress and flips me completely over. Leaning completely at a ninety-degree angle on the bed. Feet on the floor. He stretches my arms in front of me on the bed and demands that I keep them there.

"Don't move."

He lifts my dress and smacks me on one ass cheek.

Whack!

And then the other.

I hear him open a drawer and pull out a little foil condom packet. He puts the condom near my mouth and demands that I help him open it with my teeth. I can tell that he is stroking his dick with his other free hand. He is going to fuck me senseless with Sarah in the other room, and I'm going to let him.

"Tear it open."

There's no turning back at this point, but I ask the question anyway.

"What about Sarah?"

"Did you honestly believe any of that shit about us living together?" he snaps.

"Yes."

"That's your fucking problem. You always forgot what you meant to me. I ended it with her the second you left the lounge. Hell, it was over the second you walked in there."

"But she's here tonight."

"We were never serious. We're friends. She was putting on an act for you the other day, and I let her, because I wanted to see you hurt. But now, baby, I want to see you come."

Mason slides the condom on his dick and takes little time to slide it hard into my pussy without warning. He grips my hair and pulls back on it like the reins of a horse as he continues to pound me from behind with punishing strokes until it's clear that I'm about to come.

Then he suddenly pulls out.

"I want to see your face when you fall apart for me. I haven't seen it in so long. You've been a bad girl keeping what's mine from me all of this time, Olivia. What am I going to do about it?"

He gets on the bed and sits against the headboard.

"I know just the thing ... you're going to ride me."

I eagerly climb on the bed, straddle Mason, and start to lower myself slowly onto his dick. This position has never been easy for us because of his girth, but I think that's the point. This is supposed to be both a punishment and a reward.

And I gladly accept both.

"That's it." His eyes close in bliss as he lowers the zipper of my dress. "Let me get all the way in there. Work your pussy faster, baby."

I start to get in a groove as I lean my palms

against the wall above his head and ride him like a pro. Once I get wet enough, things get a little easier. It's like I haven't missed a beat. I remember what he likes, and I remember what to do.

"Dammit, Olivia, you feel so good."

He opens his eyes to find me staring into them.

Panting.

Grinding.

Falling for him all over again.

"Be brave, baby. What else do you want to say to me?"

He slips the top of my dress down to my waist, reaches for one of my breasts, and starts sucking on it.

"I love you."

"I know, babe."

"I'm sorry."

"You better be."

"I can't let you go."

"Keep riding me like this and I won't ever let you out of this fucking room."

We both start laughing.

This is what I missed.

Us together.

Us happy.

I lean back and continue to work his length. In

this position he takes his thumb and starts to rub out my clit as I fuck him. This drives him crazy and me insane. I increase my speed and so does he.

"I'm coming!" I announce.

"Not yet."

"Why?!" I demand to know angrily.

I'm right on the precipice of a monumental orgasm.

"Because I fucking said so."

He abandons my clit and uses both of his hands to caress then pinch my nipples, while he simultaneously slides his tongue inside of my mouth, and it only takes another second for me to come loud and hard with his own orgasm quickly chasing behind mine.

He chuckles after we finally come down and we finish the kiss.

"You did not follow directions. I said not to come yet."

"I bet that I can do better next time," I say smiling against his chest.

"What are we betting for?" he asks. "Dinner? Cash?"

"For the rest of our lives, Diesel."

"Now that's a bet I'm willing to gamble on, Jersey girl. Let's make it double or nothing!"

American Sports Network

"The Nighthawk stadium is on fire tonight, Rowena."

"It sure is, Dan."

"The crowd is really into this conference final now that the Nighthawks have tied things up."

"This is for all the marbles. Whoever wins this tonight goes to the big dance in Houston."

"I think the key factor in tonight's win is going to be if AJ can get Bridgewater the ball one more time. Bridgewater hasn't made any mistakes tonight and he's making what seems like impossible catches."

"So true."

"Here we go, Rowena! AJ just aired it out and,

oh my gosh, Bridgewater caught it in a one hand catch! Touchdown!"

"What an amazing catch!"

"Were both of his feet in bounds?"

"They looked like they were to me, Dan. Refs are double checking as they do all touchdown plays. They were in! It's a touchdown."

"Incredible ball game tonight and there you have it folks. The New York Nighthawks will be representing the NFC in this year's Super Bowl down in Houston, Texas."

"What a game that's going to be. Let's cut down to the field and see who Pam can grab an interview with."

"Hi Bill and Rowena. I'm here with Nighthawks Wide Receiver, Mason Bridgewater. The man they call Diesel. You had an extraordinary game tonight. How do you feel now that you're headed to the Superbowl in February?"

"I feel absolutely amazing. I've wanted and worked for this for so long and it's finally here. We still have more work to do, and another game to get ready for, but I just want to enjoy this moment for now."

"As you should. You deserve it. Lots of injuries, a

mid-season trade to New York, and now you're going to the big dance."

"I want to say hi and a big thanks to my mom and dad, my uncle Quincy, everyone back in Bear Springs, and most of all to my best friend and fiancee–Olivia. We did it, baby!"

"Oops, wait, did you see that Bill and Rowena?"

"We sure did."

"That was adorable. Mason just stood in the middle of the field with his arms wide open as his fiancee ran and jumped into them."

"How'd she get her legs that high around his waist? You think they practiced that?"

Laughter

"They've got a lot to celebrate. An upcoming wedding, a Super Bowl appearance, and a brand new five year, fifty-million dollar contract for Bridgewater that's in the works."

"What a huge turnaround from where Bridgewater was a few short seasons ago. From a risky trade to the Nighthawk's most valuable player."

"That's what's magical about the game. Anything is possible!"

If someone had told me that this was going to be my life, I wouldn't have believed them. I'm dancing with a Super Bowl champion who happens to be my new husband, along the Bear Springs Creek, under a large gazebo covered in hundreds of lights.

Best of all, we are being serenaded by the original Thunder Road with Max Lennox on lead. My favorite boy in the band. It's like every fantasy I ever had about them as a kid. A pure fairytale.

"Tell me I was doing drugs when I read on the credits that this song he's singing is six minutes long."

"What kind of husband hires a singer to serenade her and then talks shit about it the entire time?"

"I'm just saying. I never understood what you saw in these dudes, especially the one singing right now."

"It's not for you to understand. Your only job is to fulfill my every wish and to be quiet while I enjoy this song."

"That's two jobs."

I jab my new husband gently in the abs. It's fine. They're rock hard anyway and it doesn't faze him a bit.

Mason holds me closer as we sway to one of my favorite songs in the world–*Love In Color*. I think about how he's been a part of my life for so long and how he's been there for so many of my firsts in life and I'm grateful. Grateful that he's been there for me through thick and thin, and grateful that we have now testified in front of family, friends, and God that we will always be there for each other. That we love each other and always will.

After the group finishes their song, and takes their bow, that's when I decide that this is the perfect time to turn Mason's own words back around on him and give him my surprise.

"Do you trust me, Mason?"

He smiles and runs a finger down the side of my face.

"With my life."

"With your heart?"

"With all of me."

"Then I have a secret to share with you."

"What is it, babe?"

"Let's go cut the wedding cake first."

The wedding party and guests are all sitting under the huge white tents we rented for the day. I signal to Kira, my maid of honor, that we are ready to cut the cake. She grabs the mic and makes an announcement.

"The lovely bride and groom are ready to cut the cake. As with many things about this couple, the cutting of the cake will be non-traditional."

"What does she mean?" Mason asks.

"Shh, stop asking questions and wait for it."

"Will the groom place his hand on top of the bride's and cut the first piece of cake please?"

Mason takes my hand and the cake knife and we begin to slice together.

I laugh at him because I think he's waiting for a bird to fly out or something, but it's nothing like that. That's not the surprise. We cut the second slice until we have a wedge of cake to pull out and feed each other.

"*Oh*, that's what she means. It's a pink cake inside."

"Uh-huh, and?"

"You like the colors pink as well as brown now."

"Yes, I do, but what else?"

"Aaah, the dress you wore to The Harvest Dance was pink."

"Yes." I almost roll my eyes.

"And the dress you wore to the housewarming was pink?"

"You're totally overthinking this and missing the entire point. Aren't you the smart one?"

"Then what's the point?"

"It's a gender reveal, idiot," Kira blurts out.

"A what?"

"That's right ladies and gentlemen," Kira announces on the mic. "Our favorite couple is expecting a baby girl this summer. Can we give them a round of applause please!"

"A what?!" Mason exclaims as he lifts me off the ground.

"We're having a girl." I repeat the good news.

Excited that he is so happy.

We've known about the baby for a little while but I've been keeping the gender under wraps from Mason until today.

He kisses me passionately on the mouth.

"Thank you, Olivia."

"Eh, you did half the work."

"I guess I take my job seriously."

I wrap my arms around his waist, look up into his dreamy eyes, and consider how lucky I am to have married my best friend.

"She's going to love football you know."

"Just like her mommy does. In fact, I wouldn't be surprised if she becomes the first female player in the league."

"Remember you said that." I smile.

"You've got the rest of our lives to remind me, Jersey Girl. The rest of our lives."

Diesel is the best friend and boy next door who got away, but **JETT** is the superstar quarterback with a chip on his shoulder.

Watch the sparks fly when he meets a heartbroken pediatrician in a bar who **hasn't got a clue** who he is.

Devour this sweet and sexy blind date romance tonight.

TAP TO DOWNLOAD JETT

ADRIENNE

I was a fortunate child.

Raised by two parents who were genuinely in love with each other, it was normal for me to see them laugh, hug and kiss each other all the time. To be clear, they weren't inappropriately demonstrative in front of me, but they were tastefully affectionate and everyone could see that they truly enjoyed each other's company and definitely were in love with each other. They were best friends until the day my father died and watching their interaction with each other deeply influenced me. It's probably why I've loved little boys ever since I can remember. I wanted a boy to love me just like my father loved my mother.

I know… it was a complete setup for failure. Let me give you an example.

In Kindergarten, I befriended a boy named Brad Hines. He was the funniest kid in school who always wore a super cool Mickey Mouse ringer t-shirt and had chewy fruit snacks in his lunchbox. He often traded me his fruit chews for my red delicious apples, and I knew it had to be because he liked me. Why else would anyone want an apple instead of those yummy candy-like fruit chews?

It had to be love.

But if it was love, it confused me.

Brad would sit next to me on the class carpet squares during music class but never played with me during recess. We traded our snacks during lunch period, but he never ate lunch *with* me. He cheered me on when we played organized games like Duck, Duck Goose, but he never picked me to be the Goose. Why wouldn't he pick me? It made little sense to my five-year-old brain.

This confusing relationship of ours went on until the end of third grade, when he and his family unceremoniously moved away from New York. They gave the students in the class no heads up about it; so instead I showed up for the first day of fourth grade in my brand new green dress and Brad wasn't there.

That would be the anticlimactic end of our friendship.

It wouldn't be until years later that I'd realize how significant the nature of that childhood crush impacted me. As I matured, I realized that Brad only saw me like any other kid in school. I was a classroom friend. That's it. It was me who completely romanticized the relationship because I desperately wanted to mimic what I grew up seeing.

But by this time, the damage was done.

The hurt I felt by his "rejection" of me would take root and become the foundation for all of my relationships with boys and eventually men.

I wanted them to love me, but their actions confused me. I wanted one to be my best friend, yet I didn't know how to effectively communicate with them. And most of all, I expected a man to share his deepest secrets with me, yet I didn't trust them.

Each relationship failure battered my self-esteem, and so I sought to bolster it with hard work and dedication in other areas of my life. I studied hard, played very little, worked out excessively and slept the bare minimum. Even with all of my professional success though, there was one thing that continued to elude me.

Love.

But all of that was about to change.

The moment I met him.

Ready To Find Out What Happens Next?
DOWNLOAD JETT NOW

The Masterson Series

Devour this addictive series about the possessive bad boy, Roman Masterson, who falls hard and fast for the girl he's promised his family to protect.

Masterson

Masterson Unleashed

Masterson In Love

Masterson Made

Joseph Loves Juliette

Masterson Box Set

Masterson Next Generation Series

The crazy hot fruit doesn't fall far from the tree. Dive into this second generation of Masterson men!

Knox - Knox & Gigi
Bronx - Bronx & Karma
Seven - Coming soon!

The King Brothers Series

Dive into this series of interconnected standalones featuring 3 alpha hot brothers and the women they lay claim to without apology.

Claimed - Camden & Jade
Indebted - Cutter & Sloan
Broken - Stone & Tiny
Promised - All King Brothers
King Brothers Box Set

The Nighthawk Series

Sexy & sweet sports romances set in the professional world of football. All standalones.

Saint - Saint & Sabrina
Wolf - Cooper & Ursula
Diesel - Mason & Olivia
Jett - Jett & Adrienne
Rush - Rush & Mia
Freak - Freak & Willow
Brick - Brick & Kaya
Dak - Coming soon

MY VIP LIST (Get the nitty gritty)
I have a VIP Reader mailing list. I only send free books, new release, sales or special giveaway info to this group. No spam. Please join here: http://LisaLangBlakeney.com/VIP

MY PRIVATE FAN GROUP (Casual fun)
Join my private Fan Group on Facebook also known as my "Romance Ninja Warriors" where I share all things new going on, celebrate birthdays, post teasers, yummy pics, giveaways and just chit chat.
http://LisaLangBlakeney.com/community

ABOUT THE AUTHOR

Lisa Lang Blakeney is a USA Today Bestselling author of contemporary romance sold in more than 28 countries. Worried that her fellow PTO moms might disapprove, she wrote and published her steamy debut novel Masterson under a different title and pen name in August of 2015.

Thanks to strong reader support of her alpha male character, Roman Masterson, she was encouraged to continue with the series and published the entire Masterson Trilogy the following year. She hasn't looked back since and continues to write novels featuring strong alpha men and the smart women they seek to claim.

A romance junkie for sure, you can find Lisa watching a romantic comedy, reading a romance novel, or writing one of her own most days of the week. If she's not doing that, she's outside in the garden tending to her roses.

Lisa is the wife of one alpha (whom she met in college), mother to four girls, and two labradoodles. Get news on releases, sales and giveaways when you become one of Lisa's VIP readers at : http://LisaLangBlakeney.com/VIP

facebook.com/authorlisalangblakeney

twitter.com/LisaLangWrites

instagram.com/LisaLangBlakeney

amazon.com/author/lisalangblakeney

bookbub.com/authors/lisa-lang-blakeney

goodreads.com/Lisa_Lang_Blakeney

pinterest.com/lisalangwrites

tiktok.com/@lisalangblakeney

patreon.com/lisalangblakeney